SYMPHONY OF RUIN

ALSO BY CHRISTINA LAY

Death is a Star
ShadowSpinners: A Collection of Dark Tales (editor)

SYMPHONY OF RUIN

A LABYRINTH OF SOULS NOVEL

BY

CHRISTINA LAY

ShadowSpinners Press

Cover art by Josephe Vandel.
Book design by Matthew Lowes.

ShadowSpinners Press
shadowspinnerspress.com

Typeset in
Minion Pro by Robert Slimbach
and IM FELL Double Pica by Igino Marini.
The Fell Types are digitally reproduced
by Igino Marini, www.iginomarini.com.

Learn more about
the Labyrinth of Souls game at
matthewlowes.com/games.

Editor's Preface

Dungeon Solitaire: Labyrinth of Souls is a fantasy game for tarot cards, written by Matthew Lowes and Illustrated by Josephe Vandel. In the game you defeat monsters, disarm traps, open doors, and explore mazes as you delve the depths of a dangerous dungeon. Along the way you collect treasure and magic items, gain skills, and gather companions.

Now ShadowSpinners Press is publishing this and other stand-alone novels inspired by the game. Each *Labyrinth of Souls* novel features a journey into a unique vision of the underworld.

The Labyrinth of Souls is more than an ancient ruin filled with monsters, trapped treasure, and the lost tombs of bygone kings. It is a manifestation of a mythic underworld, existing at a crossroads between people and cultures, between time and space, between the physical world and the deepest reaches of the psyche. It is a dark mirror held up to human experience, in which you may find your dreams ... or your doom. Entrances to this realm can appear in any time period, in any location. There are innumerable reasons why a person may enter, but it is a place antagonistic to those who do, a place where monsters dwell, with obstacles and illusions to waylay adventurers, and whose very walls can be a force of corruption. It is a haunted place, ever at the edge of sanity.

SYMPHONY OF RUIN

1

DEATH MADE ITS NIGHTLY ROUNDS of the old quarter. Skeletal toes scraped the cobblestones and bones rattled in the keening wind blowing down from the steppes. The scythe of oblivion spared no one; man, woman or child might be snatched. This alone was reason enough to raid Master Marek's pantry and Remy could think of several others as he cleared a space on the long table against the wall. He placed one knee on the well-worn surface and tested its strength. The table wobbled only slightly on uneven legs.

"Are you sure this is a good idea?" his friend Glyn asked from behind him.

"Not only is it good, it is excellent. Top notch. One of the best I've ever had." Remy grabbed at the row of shelves to steady himself as he climbed up. The collection of bottles and jars rattled alarmingly. He paused as they settled. Nothing fell except a tuft of what looked like dried moss.

When he'd first moved in, Remy would have needed to use a footstool to reach the tabletop and he'd have to stand on the rickety table to reach Marek's stash of quality liquor. Now if he stretched full length, he could finger the row of colored glass bottles on the top shelf while still on his knees.

Some of the bottles were filled with dyed water. He knew this because he was the one who'd drained and refilled them. His master never noticed because Marek rarely partook of the odd offerings of beet brandy, moss wine, crabapple cider and so on that his clients sometimes paid him with. No, Marek reserved his imbibing for the good stuff in the cut crystal decanter, an amber brandy he shared with Remy on Winter's solstice, and then only by the wee thimble full.

Remy remembered its heat coating his throat, the flavors of caramel, loam and wealth, and the comforting affect a mere sip had on his state of mind. That was what he needed now—comfort. Glyn had just brought him the news of their mate Abernath's death. Abernath, a robust young man of seventeen years—the same age as Remy and Glyn—had been found dead in an alley the night before without a fresh mark on him.

Remy's long fingers tweezed the decanter toward the edge of the shelf. Glyn took an audible breath, sucking air out of the room in the process, braced to flee at the first hint of disaster. Glyn would rather face death than Master Marek in a rage.

"Marek is in the Giant Mountains," Remy assured him, voice a little pinched from the effort of stretching to his full length and a tiny bit beyond. "I've had no word from him for weeks. He's not about to pop up in the middle of the night with no notice. He likes his fire to be lit and his supper warm when he returns from a long trip." The decanter tipped forward and Remy caught it with his other hand. As he eased back his sleeve caught on a jutting handle and brought a little pot thudding to the tabletop. The pottery cracked. Something black and viscous oozed out.

"Ox balls," Remy muttered, and clambered down from the table.

"What is that?" Glyn backed up as if a jinn might spring forth from the ooze.

"Nothing to worry about," Remy said. He gave the scratch marks on the lid a closer look. *Ox balls and a pig's poker to boot.* "Nothing to worry about immediately anyway. Come on. Where's your cup?"

He nudged the fretful Glyn out of Marek's workspace and into the tiny front room, which contained the flickering hearth, two heavy oak chairs facing the fire, a table to eat and write at, and not much else. Well, not much except for the two thousand three hundred and ninety seven books, journals, and loose bound collections of papers stuffed into every nook, cranny, shelf, and bit of floor space. The books weighted the walls down, seeming to draw them forward to the brink of collapse. They pressed in on Remy, taunting him with all the things they knew and he didn't, because he couldn't read Latin, Giant, or Fae. He'd only learned to read his own language a few years ago, when Marek took him on as apprentice.

He ignored the glowering spines of inscrutable tomes and removed the stopper from the decanter. A warm, spicy scent filled his nostrils. He poured a wee dram into Glyn's upraised cup, then a little more. He wasn't stingy like Marek. Remy poured himself a generous measure, set the decanter on the table and raised his cup in a toast.

"To Abernath." His eyes teared a little and he swiped them away with the back of his wrist. "And Master Marek. May his journey be safe and fruitful."

"And may he return soon," Glyn added, "But not too soon."

They clacked their stoneware cups together and took cautious sips. Nothing like the gulping they did when they had a penny to spare and visited the riverside public house where beer was cheaper than clean water.

The warmth he remembered glided through Remy's blood and softened his stiff bones. Glyn coughed, and kept on coughing.

"It burns!" he said, blue eyes watering. Remy looked at his friend with a knowing sympathy. Glyn was a scrawny wisp of a thing, with stringy brown hair tied back in a tail, large eyes that always gave him a startled appearance, and a faint scruff of facial hair peppering his pointy chin. They used to be the same size, but regular meals had spurred Remy's growth. To his irritation, his chin remained smooth and hair-free. This fact combined with the occasional bath that revealed his once grimy hair really was black made them less interchangeable than they'd once been. Indistinct members of a dirty little tribe. Remy used to miss the anonymity, but not so much anymore. As a sneak thief, invisibility was a desirable trait. As an up and coming alchemist, it rankled.

Remy and Glyn had been pals since before Remy could remember. His first memories involved running from river wraiths with Glyn by his side. They grew up on the streets and in the old tunnels beneath the city. Glyn was still without a permanent home, but his association with Remy had added a little color to his cheeks and put some flesh on his starved bones.

"Never had the good stuff, have you?" Remy took a larger sip. "The good stuff always burns."

"It does have a pleasant taste after the feeling comes back," Glyn said, licking his lips appreciatively.

"Right. Now on to the business at hand." Remy gestured toward the two chairs facing the smoldering log on the hearth. Marek had devised a clever funnel that directed the smoke out a hole in the wall above the leaded glass window. Marek's domicile was one in a row of connected cottages clinging to the side of the hill. His windows faced east, overlooking the next row of houses below and a jumble of unlikely trees growing tenaciously from a bit of cliff too steep to build on. After a sharp drop the chaotic buildings of the riverside and wharf took over, ending abruptly at the flood wall, which was in the process of crumbling and falling into the fast flowing river. It was always in the process of crumbling, just as Marek's house was always in the process of sliding down the hill. Somehow, the old quarter kept its grip on the hillside, no matter how hard the winter rains fell or how fierce the northern winds blew.

Above it all, the castle complex, the new cathedral, and the palaces of the rich perched like vultures on a disintegrating nest.

Remy sank into Marek's chair with only the slightest unease prickling the hairs on his neck. He'd never sat in Marek's chair before. Glyn plopped down in the chair opposite with a sigh. After a moment he stuck his boots toward the fire. Remy noted the soles were more holes than leather. Bare skin showed through the worn spots.

"You have it good here, Remy," Glyn noted.

"Eh, that's true." To be plucked out of the gutters by a man as important as Marek and given a position and place to sleep was unheard of luck. Remy, a filthy, flea-infested criminal had been granted a first chance at life by some accidental miracle, for surely the gods gave not one pig's ear about his fate. So why was Remy so discontented?

Was it because after years of hard study, risking his life and eternal soul at Marek's side, he was still little more than a glorified errand boy? What magic had he done? Precious little.

While Marek was gone Remy was supposed to be filling in, taking on the simple cases of kitchen pixie infestations, troll encroachments on root cellars and the like. But when his clients learned Marek was away they sneered at Remy and announced they would wait for the master's return. They wanted no former street urchin in their house.

Even when Marek was here, when clients called, Remy was banished to his corner, where he still slept even though he'd long ago outgrown the matt Marek had provided. Once it had seemed the height of luxury to have a roof over his head and a fire to warm him. Now, sleeping on the floor made him feel like a pet dog. Remy only sat on the chair across from Marek when the master was feeling lonely, philosophical, or—after a great victory over some particularly nasty monster—friendly.

Remy swirled the last drams of his drink. "So what are we going to do about this plague?"

"We?" Glyn's voice squeaked when he was nervous, which was always. "You're the fancy conjuring man."

"Every alchemist needs an apprentice. What if I take you on as my helper, teach you a trick or two?" Remy quickly warmed to the idea of having someone else carry all the jars and pots of potions, not to mention the banishing rods, crystals, and that god-awful enchanted mace.

"And what would my pay be?" Glyn's expression sharpened, ever the street dweller on the prowl for coin. Remy grinned.

"Food. Liquor." He lofted his cup. "A warm place to sleep until Marek returns."

"You've given me that already," Glyn said. "Not much of a businessman, are you?"

Remy scowled, then laughed. "If we rid the city of the scourge, there will be a hefty reward. I'll give you a percentage, say ten percent."

"Say twenty." Glyn leaned forward, arm on his chair. The brandy had emboldened him, Remy decided.

"Thirteen."

"Fifteen and a pair of wool socks."

"Done." They drank to it. Remy rose to retrieve the decanter and pour them another dram or two. He settled the decanter on the wooden floor next to his chair. "Now, down to business." He thought of how Marek approached any difficult case, with reflection and the tedious poring over of books. Most of the books were closed to Remy, but he could reflect with the best of them.

He steepled his fingers in front of his lips. "What do we know of this plague?"

"Seven dead. All wharf dwellers. All found stone dead in the morning without a scratch. Skin pale and waxy as sacramental candles, eyes frozen open in terror. Last thing they saw was death standin' over them, scythe gleaming in the moonlight."

"Now you're just repeating gossip, Glyn. You weren't there, after all, were you?"

"I saw the sailor when they hauled him out of his boat. Stiff as an oar, fingers curled like he was gonna scratch death's eyes out." Glyn mimicked the look, fingers hooked like an angry cat, mouth agape. It was an impressive rendition.

"Sounds like a blood eater victim but there've been no sightings. The old gang always knows when one of those devils are afoot."

Glyn crossed himself even though he was no Christian. "No," he said, and downed his drink in one gulp. The burn didn't seem to bother him anymore.

"So is it a sickness like the docs are saying, or some new monster attack?" Remy mused.

"Hell if I know!"

"Settle down. I'm just thinking out loud, like Marek does." Remy stared into the fire. He preferred monsters to illness. Monsters were solid demons one could face. Sickness was invisible and tricky to identify, unless of course it was one of the annual plagues that swept through the city's hovels. This manner of death was entirely unheard of though.

"We're going to have to look at the bodies."

"I'm going to need more than socks to go into the catacombs!"

"Too late. We have a verbal contract. And we drank on it, so it's legal."

Glyn snorted. Laws meant nothing to the likes of him, or Remy either, to be truthful.

"Besides," Remy said, "they won't have carried them in far, just dumped them right in an opening. It's so cold now they'll freeze solid. Won't have to stuff them down until spring. I know how those grave men work."

Remy wasn't any happier than Glyn about a trip to the underground cemetery, but that's where their investigations often started. He'd almost gotten over the sweaty attacks of panic he suffered whenever they approached one of the openings down at the water line. But he'd never gone without Marek before.

"Isn't there something in all these books that will tell you what's killing these folk?" Glyn asked.

"Not until I have more facts. Then I can consult the books." Remy poured Glyn another drink to distract him from the accursed books. He'd never admitted that he couldn't read most of them, and might have even implied, at some point when they'd had too much beer and were full of themselves after successfully flirting with the overfed barmaids at the public house, that he'd read a good portion of them.

Glyn looked up to him. Others in the old gang thought Remy had become soft and snooty living in a real house, but Glyn understood the value of improving one's self, unlike the others who cared only for robbing and conning enough to fill their bellies. Still, they were Remy's gang. He'd grown up with them, so he tolerated their shortcomings with admirable self-restraint.

Feeling the need to demonstrate his wisdom, Remy stood. The floor shifted and for an instant he feared the house had finally started to slide off its perch, but it was only his brain that was sliding around. He steadied himself and reached for an impressive red book with gilded curlicue writing along the spine.

He opened it and recognized the squiggles on the page as Fae, the most confounding of all the magical languages.

"Here for instance, in Crumberry's Collection of … er … Great Fairy Wisdom, there is laid out a series of counter spells to all sorts of malevolent enchantments, but they are very specific, so I'll have to check for signs of a curse, as well as monster energy or indications of physical illness."

Glyn's eyelids drooped and his smile was lopsided, but he looked properly impressed. "Aren't you the fancy one?" he said, but with pride rather than mockery.

"Very fancy," Remy agreed. He stood straighter, book balanced in the crook of his elbow and adjusted his wool tunic. It was plain and grey and too big, being purchased from Anton the butcher who'd grown too fat for it, but it was a far cry nicer than the rags he used to wear. He wore thick leggings tucked into nice leather boots without holes, and he felt a twinge of guilt for his whiny mewling about respect. He couldn't eat respect, or wrap it around him to keep him warm.

He was of an age now where survival on the streets grew more difficult. Even though the urchins were roundly despised, the citizens of the city gave a grudging bit of leeway to the feral children scrounging around in the gutters. Pickpockets and beggars under the age of seven were rarely executed. Between the ages of eight and facial hair, or large breasts in the case of girls, a street kid was still more likely to be assigned to hard labor than a walk to the gallows when they were arrested. Once an urchin became a man, as Remy recently had, all forgiveness fell away. No shopkeeper tossed him a crust of dry bread now. Soldiers eyed him as a possible recruit into their miserable foot brigades and gang leaders looked at him as a rival and a threat. Or they would, if not for the protection of Marek.

Remy in turn felt the need to pass his luck on to his old pals, no matter what they thought of him. "But it's not about being fancy," he said. "It's about being smart. Books can stuff your head full of knowing, but they can't make you smart. You can only get that by living."

"Goin' to the catacombs doesn't sound smart to me," Glyn said.

"Sometimes you have to be brave instead of smart," Remy said. "Or as well as, I mean."

"Read me something." Glyn yawned and curled his legs up beside him in the chair. He wrapped his arms around his knees and rested a cheek on his thighs. Remy recognized the posture. He still slept the same way himself, curled into a tight shell.

Remy flipped through the impressive book in his arms. He could make up anything. Glyn would be asleep in moments. He ran his fingers along the lines in the book and recalled Marek's voice reading aloud in Fae. Illustrations of flowers and vines decorated the borders. Strange little creatures peeped out at him, so cunningly rendered they almost appeared to move.

He stared hard at the words, willing them to give up their sounds, if not their meaning. A snatch of Fae rose to his mind and out his mouth.

"*Folay ray o tay sonnat emmer fam lay toon.*" The phrase sounded right to his tipsy ears. Tipsy ears. He giggled, imagining a fairy with pointy ears that flopped over when the fairy had too much brandy.

"Whassit?" Glyn mumbled, head against the back of the chair, eyes closed.

Christina Lay

Remy repeated the line. When had Marek chanted those words? When he'd believed Remy to be asleep in the corner. Remy had a vision of Marek in his chair before a dwindling fire, back to Remy, chanting, moonlight streaming in the windows. Remy said the words one more time. All the hairs on his neck stood on end and the sky outside darkened, as if thick clouds had snuffed out the moon. Remy shivered and put the book back on the shelf. Not a good idea to fool with fae magic, even if only partly remembered.

"I'll tell our fortune," he said, and removed a small box from a lower shelf. He opened it and removed a deck of faded, dog-eared cards. There were no words to read, only pictures. Marek had demonstrated them once, while dismissing them as a vulgar method of popular magic. Washer women and bone weavers used them to frighten children, and street magicians sold false fortunes to the gullible.

"Fortune. I like the sound of that," Glyn mumbled, chin bobbing to his chest.

Remy sat down and pulled the little table beside Marek's chair in front of him. He shuffled the cards and spread them into a fan. "Pick one."

Glyn pawed one free, knocking a few from Remy's hands in the process, and held it close to his face, squinting. Remy snatched it from him and put it face up on the table. It showed a young man in silly clothes about to step off a cliff.

"Ha! The Fool. That's you for sure."

Glyn snorted. "No, that's you 'bout to wander into the catacombs."

Remy frowned. "No. You picked it. It's your fortune." On second thought, Remy didn't find the card so amusing. It might mean Glyn was a fool for following Remy.

Glyn yawned. "You pick one."

Remy reshuffled the remaining cards and flipped one over. He grinned when he saw what it was. "The Magician. That's clearly me. Look at us." He put The Fool and The Magician side by side.

"And what are those fine gents up to?" Glyn asked. Remy would have preferred to just stare at The Magician and imagine his future greatness, but two cards did not a fortune tell. He plucked out a third card and tossed it down.

The card showed a bunch of swords stuck in a barren ground. Remy counted them. "The ten of swords."

"What good are ten swords?"

"Plenty. Ten is the number of completion. This card shows how after fighting a hard battle, we'll come home victorious with all the swords."

"And we can sell them? Trade them in for beer and bread?"

"Exactly." Remy picked up the ten of swords. It was a dreary card, but the sword cards often were. One didn't come to greatness by strolling through fields of lilacs.

Glyn started to snore. Remy shuffled away the other cards, but left The Magician sitting on the table. Was it Remy, or Marek? Remy had drawn it. He would be the magician one day. He picked it up and held it close to his face. The image didn't want to hold still. Remy shook his head, then focused on the hooded figure. He whispered the Fae words again, the ones that had stirred some hidden magic.

The air in the room grew frigid, the fire dancing in a sudden gust.

A figure shimmered to life in the middle of the room, a shadowy reflection of the image on the card.

"Who's there?" the apparition whispered. "Don't hide now. I can feel you."

Remy leapt to his feet and stumbled away from the fire, away from its light.

The figure held up a lantern and peered around the room. "This place looks familiar. Am I dreaming of home again?"

The light lit his face. Remy stifled a cry of surprise. It was Marek.

"Hmmm. I know you're out there in this interminable fog. Have you nothing to say?"

Remy remained immobile. Marek would not appreciate Remy fooling with magic this powerful. Unguided. Drunk. No. No good would come of this.

Marek lifted his head and sniffed. "What's that foul odor?"

Remy sniffed as well. Only then did he notice a tendril of smoke curling out of the pantry.

"Ox balls!" he shouted. This apparently undid the spell, because Marek disappeared with nary a ripple. Remy dashed into the pantry to find the cracked pot foaming and a large black burn spreading across the table.

"By the king's beard, what a mess!" He snatched his blanket from the corner and threw it over the pot, momentarily smothering the smoke. His eyes watered and his throat burned as he searched the shelves for a dampening agent. Finally his groping hands landed on a jar of powdered seashells. He removed the blanket and dumped the contents of the jar on the burn, which still ate away at the wood. After gingerly wrapping the pot in his only blanket, he stuffed it into a metal pail and sat it outside the front door. Throwing open all the windows, he fanned away the smoke as best he could.

A tendril of smoke crystallized in the freezing air as it spiraled toward the sliver moon. Remy leaned out the window and breathed deep. Marek would kill him if he ever found out. *When* he found out. There was no hiding the damage and Remy couldn't afford to buy a whole new table. Oh, well. Nothing to be done about it now. When his face was completely numbed by cold, Remy pulled back and shut the window.

Glyn hadn't twitched during the entire affair, though his nostrils were blackened and he sneezed in his sleep. He'd missed his chance to see Remy's impressive abilities at work.

"Tomorrow you'll see more impressive things than Marek summoning," Remy assured his sleeping friend. Now that the irritation of the burning table had passed, he allowed himself to be impressed with what he'd done. He'd called up Marek without even trying. Marek who was far away in the Giant Mountains.

He yawned and thought about Marek's bed upstairs in the cramped attic. The feather mattress was luxuriously soft. Remy had experimented with lying on it when Marek was gone one day, but it had felt too dangerous, like a trap he might never escape from.

He sighed and stumbled over to his corner, where he curled up every night. Although dead tired and more than a little drunk, he stood swaying in front of the window. Way down on the riverside, he spotted a hooded figure lofting a scythe. He blinked and the image was gone.

A dream, and he'd probably dreamed Marek as well. Of course he had. Marek's brandy was too rich for his urchin blood. He gave in to the pull of exhaustion and settled in on his mat, curled up into a tight bony shell, missing his blanket rather keenly.

2

THE MOUTH OF THE CATACOMB gusted dank, fetid air. A persistent wind howled and keened deep in the belly of the hillside, playing the maze of tunnels like a massive organ made of bones and rubble.

Remy's head throbbed and his throat was parched. Brandy was a much harsher mistress than beer, he decided.

"Are you sure this is a good idea?" Glyn asked. He also looked unhappy, his wide eyes bleary and his posture concave, as if his head and shoulders were too heavy a burden to bear.

Remy tried to muster a show of enthusiasm, but there was really no selling a trip into the catacombs as a good idea. Only a necessary one.

"There's no way around it if we want to stop this plague."

"Can't we wait for Master Marek?"

"And let how many more people die?" Remy turned on his friend, away from the abyss of the tunnel. "I have no idea when he'll be back. He's already overdue, with no word of his return. He might have been cooked into a giant's stew for all I know." Remy instantly regretted his words. There was no reason to suspect anything dire had befallen his master and there was no point in begging after bad news.

Glyn frowned and did not looked convinced. Remy's determination was fading fast as well. Why not wait for Marek? He bundled his thin cloak tighter around him. "We only need to go in as far as the last few burials."

The tunnels weren't real catacombs, or at least that hadn't been the original intention. The hill on which the city was founded was only partially natural. Over the centuries, it had grown higher as conquerors built upon the crushed remains of the conquered. The crowning castle and cathedral stood upon a mountain of ruins. In some places, old rooms and passageways were still in use as cellars and conduits, but the deeper one went, the more hazardous and impenetrable they became. At the water's edge, the tunnels served as a convenient storage place for the dead during the winter, when the ground in the fields beyond the city froze to a stone-like consistency. But eventually, the reburial of the poor stopped happening, and the grave men left frozen corpses in what became a subterranean cemetery of unknown depth. Every few years, floods washed away the recently stowed, clearing out room for more.

As a street urchin, Remy had explored endless lengths of the tunnels and intriguing ruins, but like everyone else, stayed away from the catacombs. When the winter winds blew, as they did now, the cemetery moaned and howled. People said it was the song of the dead, lamenting their fate.

"How about a beer first?" Remy asked. Glyn nodded enthusiastically and as one they turned to the narrow stone steps carved into the flood wall. But at the same time, a tumult from above reached them. Kettle pots serving as drums pounded, and the tell-tale bell of the grave men rang out.

"Another death?" Remy mused, though he knew full well what it was when old Silas the grave man appeared at the top of the wall, shaking his bell. Silas looked as though he'd spent a few nights in a fresh grave himself, pale, dirty, and slightly translucent in the harsh light of an overcast dawn. The clouds above formed a flat lid that glowed at the edges, casting a pall over the little processional as it made its precarious way down the stone steps.

First came Silas in his grubby burial clothes, then his helper bearing the front end of a canvas stretched between poles. On the canvas lay the corpse, covered with a scrap of dirty cloth. Bartow the beggar carried the back end, followed by the mourners.

Remy's heart tightened when he realized he knew them. Saucy Sadie and Melina were old mates of his.

The processional somehow reached the brick quay without dumping the body into the river and came to a halt.

"What're you two doin' here?" Silas asked, eyeing them with suspicion.

"I've come to examine the dead on Master Marek's behalf," Remy said quickly. This earned him a grudging nod instead of the cudgel he used to get when he was nobody. "Is this a new victim of the current plague?"

"Aye." Silas shuffled back to the body and ripped the cloth aside. "Found dead in an alley." He shrugged at Sadie and Melina whose faces were red with tears. Remy braced himself and looked at the corpse. It took a moment to recognize her due to the grimace that stretched her lips unnaturally wide.

"Awww, it's Rosie!" Glyn wailed, and burst into tears himself. Remy stifled any such natural reaction he might have had, intent on appearing professional and calm, like Marek always did. Rosie, an older girl, had served as a sort of mother figure to Remy's gang, giving a helping hand to wee ones and bandaging wounds when she wasn't robbing them blind. It was a horrible thing to see the robust gang leader frozen stiff, strong fingers curled into claws, teeth bared, eyes dull as pebbles.

"When's your master coming back?" Sadie cried. "He's got to put a stop to this! Rosie was plenty healthy last night when we saw her last, weren't she, Melina?" The other girl nodded. "It ain't right, healthy people dropping dead."

"Master Marek is in the Giant Mountains, but I am in communication with him." Remy decided the lie might help stem a panic, and also get him access to more information. "I will relate my observations to him via messenger crow."

"Get on with it," Silas groused. "I don't get paid to stand here freezing my balls off."

Remy cleared his throat and approached the body as if he did this sort of thing every day. He poked Rosie's waxy, almost pewter-colored skin and drew his finger away quickly. Already she was icy-cold.

"When did you see her last?" he asked Sadie, who came to hover at his elbow, tears dried, curiosity taking over.

"After the pub shut. We parted ways at Glinsky Square. You know she was sharing a loft with Barbados the tailor but she never made it home."

"No, I didn't know that." Remy didn't keep up with the gossip as much as he used to. What a shame Rosie had died after finally securing a warm bed to sleep in. "And when was she found?"

"At the cock's first crow. Barbados went lookin' for her and found her in the alley not three houses from his place. He had to go open his shop or he'd be here himself, payin' for a spot higher off the ground so she don't get swept away a'fore spring." Sadie jutted her jaw out as if saying this might help get her friend a proper burial, though in all his days Remy had never seen a wharf dweller get put in the dirt and sprinkled with holy water.

He returned his attention to Rosie. He peered into her eyes for signs of possession, but they were stone dead. He searched her exposed skin for signs of wounds, rash or boils, but found nothing other than old scars badly healed. Rosie had been plump for a street person and there were no signs of wasting away or fever. More and more he was convinced the cause of her death was something unnatural.

Feeling the need to comment, he said, "Hers was a rigorous mort indeed."

"What's that mean?" Sadie asked, crowding him. She smelled like sewage and boiled potatoes, something he never would've noticed before.

"It means her death was sudden and swift. By the looks of her, she knew it was coming and had time to brace herself, but there was nothing she could do. This is the doing of a monster for sure."

"A murdering monster loose in the city?" Sadie cried loudly. Her question was turned into a statement by Bartow the beggar and before long the cry of murdering monster travelled up the stairs and spread across the wharf. Remy considered how it might have been a mistake to make such a pronouncement.

"I can't be certain until I see the others and hear what Master Marek has to say about my findings," he said, but no one was interested in doubt. Bartow dropped his end of the canvas and shuffled toward the stairs.

"I ain't goin' in the lair of no murderin' monster," he said. Silas cursed and glared at Remy. Remy looked at Glyn, who was weighed down with the bags, satchels and weaponry Remy would normally be the one to carry. He sighed and went to take Bartow's place, though it was beneath his dignity.

Silas's helper lurched forward and Remy was forced to follow. The cloth had slipped exposing Rosie's bare feet. She had dainty feet for a big girl. Remy wanted nothing so much as to slip warm socks on those feet, though she was long past caring.

They passed through the entrance to the tunnel. Moisture dripped on the back of Remy's neck and he shivered. Behind him, Glyn paused to spark a light crystal, one of the few baubles Remy had given him to make his friend's life a little easier. Now he was grateful for it because Silas didn't seem bothered by the thickening gloom as they travelled farther into the bowels of the hill. Large spiders skittered into holes as they passed and a flurry of bats brushed the top of their heads in a burst of panic.

These low, twisting caves had been carved out and fortified by the savage race that first laid the foundations of the city, back when people still lived in the ground instead of houses. Little was known about them other than they'd broken off from the race of giants to the north to mate with humans right after the gods trapped the sun and forced it to circle the world forever. They worshipped the winged worm coiled at the base of the world tree and practiced human sacrifice in its honor. Carvings on the ancient stones showed the serpent swallowing its victims whole, and other equally pleasant subjects.

Before long Remy couldn't see these charming carvings or anything besides Silas' back, partially lit by Glyn's crystal. Soon he began to see bodies stacked against the walls and shoved into niches. Silas stopped.

"Good enough," he said, and his helper lowered his end.

"Where?" Remy was both relieved and appalled that they'd go no deeper.

"Right there on top of the others." Silas pointed into an offshoot tunnel that had collapsed not far in. The floor was covered in corpses, three deep. "Though I suspect you'll be wantin' to feel 'em up first." He snickered and hacked up a glob of something. Remy's sense of rightness rebelled at leaving Rosie in such a place, but what else could he do? He set his end down and gestured at Glyn to bring the light closer. Glyn moved stiffly, none too eager to approach the mound of corpses.

Abernath lay on top of the pile. Remy was grateful for the bitter cold that arrested decay. Even so, a sickly sweet odor of river sewage and death thickened the air. In the summer this place would be … he swallowed down a surge of nausea and poked at Abernath's bare foot, the only bit he could reach without climbing on bodies.

"Is someone stealing their shoes?" he asked.

Silas shrugged. "No sense lettin' usable wares go to waste. Are you goin' to help us with this one? I got my breakfast to get to."

"In a minute." Remy took the crystal from Glyn and did as much of an inspection as he could of the recently departed. Their grim faces showed traces of iridescence from a fungus growing on the walls and ceilings of the tunnel. None of them revealed any signs of disease or violence. Some looked half-starved, but that was normal. They all shared an expression of horror. This monster was one who fed off fear.

If only he could see what they'd seen. He wondered if there was a spell for conjuring up a vision of the last moments of someone's life. A particularly hard gust of wind made the tunnel howl like a banshee. Long strands of Remy's hair blew across his face and he fingered them back behind his ear, shivering.

"They ain't gonna start singing to you, Remy the rat boy," Silas chuckled. Remy bristled at the use of his old nickname. No matter how methodically he tried to stamp it out, it wouldn't go away. If he could solve this puzzle and stop the deaths, the city's memory of the urchin who clubbed rats to death for a half-penny a dozen would finally be put to rest.

"One never knows what the dead might do." Remy sniffed. He handed the crystal back to Glyn and reluctantly helped Silas unload Rosie onto the pile of corpses. At least she was near friends: Abernath was a mate of hers. Lars the sailor. Misha the seamstress.

Remy recognized most of the dead, and had been friendly with more than a few. Wasn't it always this way? Death swept through the gutters and alleys of the old quarter adding misery to misery. What did the rich do with their dead? Did they ever die in the night of plague and monsters? They must, though the world above on top of the hill seemed like another dimension altogether.

"I've seen all that I can see at the moment," Remy said.

"Thank goodness!" Glyn gasped in relief and bolted out of the tunnel, taking the light with him.

"Stop!" Remy called after him. Glyn paused where the tunnel curved. A few more steps and the tunnel would have been plunged into darkness. The thought sent a shudder to the core of Remy's soul. He hated the absolute blackness of the buried ruins.

Silas chuckled again and hacked up a wad of phlegm, which he spat out a little closer to Remy's boots than was polite.

"'Fraid of being in the dark with the dead?" he asked.

"Not at all. I just noticed some interesting inscriptions." There were carvings on the wall next to where Glyn had stopped, but they meant nothing to Remy. He walked up to them anyway, pretended to study the deep hash marks, then harrumphed knowingly.

"Familiar with the tongue of the old ones, are you?" Silas asked, a tiny bit of curiosity revealing itself beneath the layers of contempt.

"Naturally. Any alchemist worth his salt peter knows the mysteries of the city's past."

"So what lies beyond the catacombs, if you be knowing so much about it?"

"Nothing lies beyond the catacombs. This is the deepest layer. The tunnels only go up."

Silas snorted. "Not what I seen," he muttered, lumbering past Remy.

Remy considered asking him about this, but what did he care about whatever caves might exist below? It had nothing to do with his current problem.

He followed and soon they stood on the quay, the dank air of the river more refreshing than usual.

Glyn stood conferring with Rosie's two friends, relating grim details of the piles of corpses and giving his impersonation of their death grimace. Even tough Sadie blanched and shivered.

A small crowd had gathered up above the flood wall. Someone poked their head over and shouted, "Catch any monsters?"

"If it's rats killing these folk, we're in good hands!" another yelled back. There was much laughter and merriment, the usual response of wharf dwellers to the small tragedies of daily life.

Remy decided not to respond. There was nothing to be gained in stirring up the rabble further. He pulled his cloak tight around his shoulders and climbed the stairs.

"Monster got your tongue?"

"When's Marek coming back?"

"Is it true there are blood eaters on the loose?"

Remy ignored them, pushing through the clutch of bodies and practically fleeing up the road to the old quarter. He had nothing to tell them.

3

PILES OF BOOKS cluttered the floor at Remy's feet. Unfurled scrolls lay across the table. No matter how long or hard he stared at them, he could not read them. The crow he'd convinced to go in search of Marek hadn't returned. He was at a dead end and had begun to regret his boldness in announcing to Glyn and the world that he would put an end to the plague.

In desperation he returned to the fortune telling cards, but no wisp of power remained in them, if there'd ever been any. A crescent moon slipped in and out of the clouds, brushing the room with ordinary shadows, and sobriety robbed Remy of his confidence.

But vulgar, common magic was all Remy really knew, so he shuffled the faded deck and spread cards face down across the table. He fingered a card. What if he really had crossed the distance and reached Marek? If he had, he shouldn't have hid but used the opportunity to pick Marek's brain. All good in hindsight. If he succeeded again, he'd be better prepared.

But he was stuck. Flummoxed. Stymied. Staring at The Magician card didn't work. He couldn't remember the Fae words that had tripped so easily off his tongue the night before. Stupid books. Why couldn't they be written more plainly, with pictures to illustrate what they meant?

He glanced sadly at the empty decanter. Liquor helped him think, helped him conjure, but moss wine and beet brandy wouldn't do the trick. They would only put him to sleep and give him a headache.

Up the hill, a carriage rattled along the cobblestones of the main road. Some noble on his way to a not-so-secret tryst, or late-night revelers returning from a party in the new quarter across the river. The rhythmic clip clop of hooves was both soothing and unsettling. No one in the old quarter owned a carriage, and it was rare to hear them passing by so late at night.

Remy tried to ignore the sound, but its sudden end jarred him more than the noise itself. He listened intently, as he imagined every wakeful ear in the quarter doing. When the horse refused to make any more indications of what it was up to, Remy subsided into his own little misery, bemoaning his ignorance and the fact that what he needed to know was hidden behind obscure scratch marks on pages. He flipped over a card and was irritated to see a fancy queen on her throne. What could such a person have to do with the death of commoners?

Boots slapped along the cobblestones now, in such an obvious attempt to be stealthy the wearers might as well have screamed their presence to the world, much like whispers in a quiet room demanded attention.

Remy swept up the cards and reshuffled. He should go to bed and begin again in the morning, but his mind wouldn't stop questioning and spinning. What had killed those people? Fright? He couldn't imagine anything fearsome enough to scare Rosie out of her body. She'd been so ornery and tough. And Abernath, though thin as bones, had been sharp and fleet of foot. Of the dead, only one had been old. The sailor had been nearly forty, but by all accounts, robust.

Remy leaned back and twirled his thumbs, sure some revelation would present itself if only he thought about it hard enough.

A sharp rap on the door jerked him upright. The slapping boots had stopped outside of Marek's house. Remy considered not answering. Late night clients always brought the worst problems. But a client was a client, and there was always hope one might stay and pay him to do some simple job even after finding out Marek was away.

He padded across the floor and pressed his ear to the door. "Who's there?" he demanded, making his voice as deep as possible.

Instead of answering the visitor knocked again, but softly, not wanting to draw the attention of the neighbors, entirely ignorant of the fact that everyone who lived in the lane must be aware of their presence by now.

Pulling back the bolt and unlatching the latch, Remy eased the door open a crack. A man-shaped bulk stood close, backlit by the dim lights from the hovels across the lane. Remy could see an eyeball peeking through half-closed shutters in Berlioz's house.

Ignoring the snoop he squinted up into the face of the knocker.

"Is this the domicile of Marek Zahrad the alchemist?" the man asked.

"Yes. What do you want at this time of night?"

The man didn't answer. He pushed against the door and sent Remy stumbling backward. The intruder filled the doorway, having to stoop as he entered, fancy velvet hat brushing the frame. He stepped across the transom and glared around the room.

He wore a black leather doublet, high shiny boots, and a long sword that dangled from a thick belt. Remy reeled back even farther, instinctively recoiling from the man's rich appearance and perfume-tinged scent. The man reeked of authority and roses.

"Call your master. We wish to have words with him."

"We?" Remy peeked around the man for companions but saw no one.

The man scowled, flared his nostrils, and turned to the door. He motioned to someone, palm raised to indicate they should wait. Remy smothered an urge to climb out the window. He'd learned long ago any interaction with nobility was bound to end poorly. While others pressed forward for a glimpse of the contessa's carriage, or got excited when a well turned-out hunting party rode by on the way to the outer gates, Remy hid or ran the other way.

The rich were like mythological creatures themselves, so far removed were they from ordinary life, more supernatural than any pixie or troll but capable of great harm when they did intrude upon reality.

"Marek isn't here," Remy said. "He's gone on important business to the Giant Mountains."

"You're his servant, are you not?"

Remy puffed up a bit. "His apprentice. Who are you?"

Again the man didn't bother to answer, barreling his way past Remy as if he were no more than a piece of furniture instead of a peaceful home dweller minding his own business.

Anyone else and Remy would've taken after them with the fire poker, but the sword at the man's belt kept him still and resentful.

The man stood in the center of the room, crowding and filling it like an ox in a hen house. His hat knocked against the roof timbers. Now that he was inside a powerful sweet smell like a whore's perfume filled the room, only without the added pungency of bodily fluids.

He wrinkled his nose, one hand on the hilt of his sword and turned a slow circle. Then he marched out again. Remy nearly had the door shut when the man's heavy paw pushed it aside again.

"It is safe to enter," he announced. He stood aside and a shadowy figure slipped in from the lane. A woman wearing a long hooded cloak entered, hand pulling its edge down to hide her face. A silver ring winked on her finger.

Remy couldn't take his eyes off her as she mimicked the movements of the man, stopping in the center of the room and turning a slow circle. Her head didn't reach the timbers but she was every bit as tall as Remy.

A second man poked his head in, glared at the other two, and pulled the door shut while remaining outside.

Remy was almost over his astonishment and on his way to irritation when the woman pushed back her hood. Her hair gleamed like polished copper. Remy had never seen such hair, nor such pale, smooth skin.

She wore layers upon layers of the finest materials—a crushed velvet dress of sage green, a dark green jacket, underskirts of creamy satin—a vision of sumptuous softness. A slipper-clad toe poked out from beneath the skirts only to disappear again. All of this frippery was covered by the forest green cloak. Gold threads along the hem sparkled in the firelight.

Remy's mouth fell open and stayed that way. He didn't care. Surely this was the contessa herself! Should he drop to his knees? Offer her a drink? Again he regretted finishing off Marek's good liquor. And to think he'd wasted it on Glyn.

"When will the alchemist return?" she asked, voice soft as a lute. Unlike her escort, she smelled nice. Remy caught the whiff of lilacs. The scent transported him back to his earliest memory—as it always did—of being held. Warm arms wrapped around him and rocked; a voice murmured in his ear; soft lips brushed his head and he glimpsed a little cottage, trees, and a lilac bush. This was Remy's only image of his life before the city, before whatever calamity had ripped him from those loving arms.

He blinked and stared.

"Perhaps he's simple?" she asked, and the man snorted.

Remy snapped out of his trance. "I don't know when Master Marek will return. He's on very important business."

"But are you not in contact with him?"

"Yes, of course," he stammered. "Would you like a seat? A drink?"

He gestured at Marek's chair and winced at the sight of his abandoned supper bowl and the mess of books around the chair. He dropped to a knee and gathered the books into his arms.

"You needn't bother. I won't linger but a moment. My name is Winifred Semple. I am a lady in waiting to one of the great ladies of the city."

Remy paused and looked up at her. This magnificent woman was a servant? He shuddered to think of how ethereal and strange her mistress must be.

He shoved his armload into the other chair and straightened, adjusting his tunic and running a hand through his tangled mess of hair.

"What can we—I—do for you, my lady?"

She gave him the same inspection she'd given the room and frowned as if being presented with inferior fabric at the dressmaker's shop. "My men tell me you've been investigating the odd deaths that have occurred of late, on behalf of your master."

"Yes, but what concern could that be to your mistress?"

"Who said it was?" she snapped, rosy lips thinning. In her pique he noticed she wasn't much older than him, a fact well disguised by her clothing and haughty bearing. "We have an urgent problem that cannot wait for Marek's return. I wish you to come with me and listen to my lady's concerns. Can you do that?"

"Right now?"

"Unless you have more pressing matters to attend." She sniffed, flaring one finely curved nostril. She glanced around with distaste. She'd probably never set a satin-clad toe inside such hovel before, unless she was often called upon to do her lady's dirty work.

Remy balked. Marek would leap at the chance to serve a noble woman but he didn't share Remy's sensible terror of those with inordinate amounts of power. While Marek dreamed of nibbling at the crusts falling from the tables of the rich, Remy thought of their dungeons and their unquestionable right to take his life if the whim struck them.

"Well?" she pressed, quirking a fine eyebrow.

To refuse was even more dangerous.

He bowed and half-curtsied, as he'd seen some women do when the count rode by on his fancy white horse.

"I am your humble servant, my lady."

She lifted her chin and eyed the door. Her escort leaped to it and flung it open.

Remy snatched his cloak from its hook and ran to follow, but the man held out a hand and stopped him.

"She will not be seen with the likes of you. Petru will guide you in a few moments."

He gave one last sneering glare at Remy and around the room before following his lady up the lane. She walked silently, the man's boots slapped and they faded away. Soon the carriage began its clopping again, back up the hill.

Remy thought this might be a good time to flee, back down to the wharf to hide out with Glyn and his old mates until whatever this was blew over, but the second man appeared out of the shadows, slapping his hands together against the growing chill of the mist.

When distance swallowed the noise of the carriage, he grunted and said, "Come along, then." He walked up the hill without looking back. Remy grabbed the long key from the hook by the door, secured the latch and hastened after his guide. A worried corner of his mind wondered if he'd ever return.

4

REMY AND HIS GUIDE seemed to be alone in the night as they climbed the stairs that wound back and forth across the hillside. From the old quarter they passed into the more respectable craftsmen's neighborhood without meeting a soul.

Their footsteps banged like drums in Remy's ears and he expected to be seized by the night watchmen at any moment. Surely someone would throw open their shutters and yell at him to go back to where he belonged, but no one molested them. His escort hunkered deep into his thick jacket and said nothing.

They climbed steadily past the narrow lanes of the merchants' quarter into the wider avenues where the government and clergy folk lived. The stairs zigzagged and occasionally Remy caught glimpses of the city over the rooftops and garden walls. The oily black river cut between the old city and the new on the far side, a scattering of stars reflected on its surface. In the twin black towers guarding each end of the bridge, lanterns of the night watchmen glowed red.

Finally they reached an elbow in the stairs and Remy knew they'd crossed into territory he shouldn't be in. The enclave of the majorly wealthy and minorly noble. Houses no longer stood cheek to cheek but were separated by gardens and wide lanes. Tilting half-timbered huts gave way to three and four story mansions. Fresh paint gleamed in intermittent lantern light. The tumult and murmur of the town below faded, broken only by the distant clop of horses' hooves and the wheezing of his guide.

"Damn I hate these trips to the sewers," the man muttered, pausing at a gate to catch his breath. Remy had no problem with the climb, though anxiety made his pulse quicken.

After a moment a guard appeared at the gate, lofting a lantern.

"Who goes—oh, it's you, Petru." He lowered the light and stepped aside, giving Remy a narrow-eyed glare.

And still they climbed, mansions expanding into palaces, more gates and guards blocking the way, until they reached a large open square at the top of the hill.

Remy had heard it described but he'd never been there. A low wall rimmed the square and he leaned out over it. He could see all the way past the edges of the city to the dark forests beyond. The darkness made it impossible to tell if the low slumping forms on the horizon were clouds or the Giant Mountains.

"Quit gawkin'," Petru mumbled. He crossed the square at a quick pace, glancing side to side, but no one was about. Remy filled his eyes with as much detail as they could absorb on this dark night. The cathedral loomed at the far end of the square, so much more imposing up close, it massive towers rearing up to scrape the stars from the sky.

The old castle where the kings once lived was a stubbier mass of dark stone and it faced off grimly against the haughty cathedral. Built in ancient times, it showed its age, crumbling around the edges and sprouting moss in its many cracks. Now the garrison lived there while the king lived in newer, less drafty accommodations nearby.

Remy and Petru bypassed the wrought iron gates that led to the main castle complex and entered the grounds through a carriage tunnel, where more guards confronted them. The guards stood aside the minute they laid eyes on Petru. His mistress must be powerful indeed, Remy thought. This didn't cheer him.

Another smaller square existed within the four high wings of this part of the castle, one of the many modern additions stuck on to the original fortress. The old ramparts and watch towers now overlooked a network of frilly palaces and government buildings, all four or five stories high, with rows upon rows of glass windows, topped with fancy coats of arms guarded by gargoyles and lions.

The spectacle was too much. Remy turned his gaze to his feet. The entire lane he lived on and all its hovels could fit into one floor of one section of one wing, with room left over for a public house or two.

Petru stopped in front of a relatively modest door and rapped softy, a rap that echoed across the silent square. Remy once again imagined all the ears perking to alertness in the hundreds of rooms overlooking the door, and felt a little better thinking of the people within as prying and curious like the folks in the lane. It made them seem slightly more human.

The door opened and they slipped in. A nearly-invisible maid closed the door and scampered off to whatever hole she hid in while waiting for her betters to sneak in at the dead of night.

Remy followed Petru through a series of chambers, one leading into another, deeper and deeper into the palace until they reached a room with four doors. They went right, and then left, and then right until Remy was completely turned around, with no outside window to give a clue as to what direction they walked in. Most of the rooms were sparsely furnished, with a porcelain fireplace in one corner, stiff chairs sitting about looking as if they might collapse if anyone ever sat in them, and elaborate wrought iron chandeliers, unlit and as gloomy as clusters of sleeping bats. Not what Remy expected at all, but it was the dead of night, no lights were lit, and this wing seemed to be unoccupied. No small baubles or knickknacks lay about that could be easily pocketed, not that Remy would do such a thing as rob his client, but it was a detail worth noticing.

Just when Remy thought they must have come full circle, they reached a staircase. Petru wearily began to climb.

"Is there no end to this place?" Remy cried. Petru turned and angrily shushed him.

"Quiet you, or I'll toss you right out a window."

If there were any windows nearby Remy might have been more worried, but as it was he was tired and beginning to feel as if the whole thing were a strange dream. Was he back home slumped over the table, Queen of Swords fortune card stuck to his cheek?

And what about that? He turned over a queen card and lo and behold, a queenly—or given her young age, princessly— woman appeared at his doorstep. He pushed aside the disquieting thought as Petru at last stopped before a door and tapped lightly.

Winifred Semple opened the door, a pretend look of surprise and consternation artfully arranged on her face.

She craned her neck to see past them into the chamber. Remy was beginning to find their caution comical, seeing as how no one was about.

Satisfied, she stood aside and gestured them in.

Given that Winifred the servant was so sumptuously turned out, Remy had expected her mistress to be nothing short of a giantess bedecked in a dress made of rubies, sporting a tall pointy crown with doves on her shoulders and roses strewn at her feet, so the old stick of a woman in a thin night gown propped up on a divan came as somewhat of a disappointment.

He approached as close as he dared, and bow-curtsied again.

The old woman turned to her servant and asked shrilly, "This is the best you could do?"

"You said you wanted nothing to do with the court alchemists," Winifred said in her defense. "This boy serves Marek Zahrad, the alchemist who rid Butcher Lane of the blood eater living there disguised as a foreign lord."

"And destroyed a fair bit of property in the process, if I remember correctly," the lady said. She pawed at a quilt in her lap, and Remy noticed her fine white fingers, smooth and unblemished as a girl's. "How old are you, boy?"

Remy stiffened his spine. "My name is Remy and I'll be eighteen years in ten months."

"Hmmm, I send for an alchemist and instead I get an overgrown street urchin. Bah, the situation is utterly hopeless. I was mad to think anyone could help me." She leaned back and closed her eyes. Remy recognized the theatrics of a manipulator and was impressed. Although the woman's hair was white and her forehead creased with wrinkles, he could tell she'd been quite the beauty. Beauty combined with wealth made for a fearsome combination.

"Please, mistress," her servant said, "Tell the boy your story. Surely once his master hears your tale he will hasten back to the city."

If there's enough coin involved, Remy thought but didn't say. And there was also the pesky detail that there'd been no response to his messenger crow sent out that morning. Who knew if the crow could even find Marek? Remy had never hired one of the annoying creatures before. It might have flown off with his money never to return. Remy would be just as happy to leave right now, as empty headed as he'd arrived.

The grand lady sighed mightily and sipped from a crystal goblet that had been on the table beside her.

"Show him," she said, "and then I will tell him what there is to tell."

Winifred looked relieved. She was probably worried about being sent back out into the night in search of reputable alchemists. There weren't many, and most of them lived in danker quarters than Marek.

She walked to a door behind the divan and Remy feared he was in for another trek though the maze-like chambers, but they went only as far as the next room. In a small bed with a high canopy, he spotted a figure. It took no training to tell the man was dead. A small candle burned on a table. Winifred picked it up and carried it closer to the dead man.

His eyes were open, mouth frozen wide in mid-scream, fingers rigid and claw-like.

"Oh," Remy said.

Winifred nodded and whispered, "It's like the others, isn't it?"

"Very similar," Remy said. He approached the corpse and poked an exposed patch of skin on the back of the hand. "How long ago did he die?"

"Five nights."

"And he's still here?" Remy asked in surprise. He detected very little odor, but that might have been due to the freezing nature of whatever killed him, or the large open windows blowing in cold air, or the overabundance of scented candles flickering throughout the bedchamber. Maybe a combination of all those things.

"My lady does not wish anyone to know. Her husband's death in such an unseemly fashion would create quite the scandal. The contessa's winter ball is this week, and my lady will not risk being uninvited."

"I see," Remy said, though he didn't see at all. "Was he found here in his bed?"

"No. He was found in another bed." Winifred reddened around the neck and cheeks.

"I see," Remy said again, and this time he did. Adultery and death, a double impoliteness to his wife. "May I speak to the owner of the bed in which he died?"

"No. That person has been escorted out of the city, never to return."

"That's most inconvenient. Did this person happen to mention if she was in the room when he died?"

"That person said she'd gone in search of a servant to bring wine. When she returned to the bed chamber, Sir Wintervale was dead." Winifred turned an even brighter shade of red, which Remy found most becoming. She looked almost like a real person when she was embarrassed.

"Wintervale, eh?" The name meant nothing to him, but he wanted to see if she might turn any redder. Realizing her error, she did.

"Never mind that!" she blurted, then lowered her voice to a whisper. "Is it true there is a murdering monster running loose in the city?"

"It's neither true nor untrue," Remy said, remembering Marek's advice to be as inscrutable as possible.

"That means you don't know," she countered.

"It means we are still gathering facts. But by the looks of things, a monster or evil spirit is the most likely cause."

"But why would a monster murder a lord, and then go down to the wharf to kill commoners?"

"Maybe the lord's blood was too rich for it?" Remy did a quick calculation and realized Winifred was right; Lord

Wintervale had been the first to die. Events, turmoil and even illnesses rarely crossed the line between the upper and lower crusts of the city, so this struck him as very odd. The initial scandal of the lord's death would be added to by its association with the unwashed rabble. Lady Wintervale had taken quite the risk to bring in someone from the outside to investigate her husband's demise. She must be afraid of something more deadly than scandal.

Remy did a little checking to make sure the lord's corpse was as unmarred and unviolated as the others. Satisfied, he headed toward the lady's chamber to hear her story.

"What?" Winifred demanded. "Aren't you going to cast any spells or throw powders around? Isn't that what alchemists do?"

"Not until I know what I'm dealing with. The wrong spell might just call back the monster."

Winifred blanched and looked nervously around the room. Remy smiled smugly. She was just as teasable as any girl, he decided, despite her fancy clothes and nice smell.

They returned to face the lady, who'd straightened herself up on the divan and was now sipping from a snifter of brandy. She didn't offer any to Remy, or ask him to sit.

"Still dead?" she asked.

Remy nodded.

"My husband was inconsiderate to his dying breath. A great man, to be sure, but unconcerned with the finer aspects of court life. It would have been so much better if he'd died in battle."

"Do you know why your husband visited the catacombs?" Remy asked.

The woman started, but recovered quickly. "What makes you think he'd go anywhere near that vile place?"

Remy had made note of the same shiny fungus he'd seen in the catacombs on Lord Wintervale's hands, and a slight dusting in his hair. But he wasn't about to admit such a mundane fact.

"I don't think. I know."

Lady Wintervale glared at him, then relented. "So your urchin has a bit of a brain after all, Winifred. You may leave us now. You too, Petru." Winifred looked disappointed, but curtsied and hurried to the door. Petru started to protest but was cut off by a wave his lady's fingers.

Once they were alone the lady sagged a bit, shoulders rounded. Clearly she didn't care what Remy thought of her posture.

"Most inconsiderate," she said again.

"Why did your husband go to the catacombs?"

"He went in search of a bauble."

"What sort of bauble?"

"Does it matter?"

"Very much. Blood eaters love gold but roundly hate silver. Witches desire emeralds more than anything. Wraiths eat pearls by the handful."

"Enough! He'd gone in search of a gold medallion that had recently been stolen from the cathedral."

"Did he find it?"

"No."

"Why did he think to look for it in the catacombs?"

"Because that's where the thief's body is. There was a slight chance it might still be on his person or near abouts."

"Lady Wintervale, that is a very important piece of information! You should have told me right away." Excitement surged through Remy. His first real clue to the nature of the monster had just been revealed.

"Who told you my name?" the lady asked sharply. Remy bit his lip, thinking fast.

"The big fellow who first knocked on my door."

"Nonsense. Gavin wouldn't be so stupid. Winifred is a sturdy girl but not very bright. I know it was her. Don't lie to me."

"If you don't lie to me, I won't lie to you," Remy said.

"You're a glib little snot, aren't you?" she scowled but went on. "If you must know, the thief was my brother-in-law. Now his ghost is lurking about. First he taunted my husband with the damage that would be done to the family name when the theft was discovered, then he frightened the poor man to death. He's clearly peeved at having his bones left in the catacombs with commoners instead of placed in the family vault."

"Why would your husband do such a thing?" Remy asked, genuinely shocked.

"I told you. Inconsiderate." The woman sipped her wine and avoided Remy's gaze.

"Lady Wintervale—"

"Oh, all right. Roderick, my husband's brother, was found dead in the old chapel, either by murder or suicide. Appalling affair. My husband had to attend to the mess quickly and so he had the grave men chuck Roderick into the catacombs."

"That was a very reckless thing to do." Remy stroked his chin. "It appears he unleashed an angry spirit. But why would your husband's brother go murdering about in the old quarter? Even dead people tend to stick to their class."

"I don't know, and I don't care. What I do care is that you banish this ghost before anyone discovers who it once was. It would reflect very badly on the house of Wintervale and hinder my son's attempts to become advisor to the king if anyone found out Sir Roderick has turned to haunting."

"The solution is simple. You must remove your brother-in-law from the catacombs and place him in the family vault."

"Impossible! No one other than the monks who found him knows Roderick is dead. They all think he's hunting in the east. Naturally my husband didn't tell anyone his brother stole the wretched medallion and got himself killed in the most unsuitable fashion. And you can't go hauling corpses out of the catacombs without drawing attention. No, you must find some potion or other to get rid of him."

"Ghost eradication is a very complicated affair, especially when the ghost is free-roaming."

"Oh, I know the swindling ways of your kind. I'll pay your fee, but be warned, I'll know if you're trying to cheat me." She wagged one of her elegant fingers at him. Remy had no clue what such a woman might consider a fair fee, but his innards warmed with greed.

"How did Sir Roderick die?"

"He bled out. Knife wound to the neck. And before you ask, I don't know what he was doing in the chapel in the first place or anything else about the sordid mess. My husband seemed to know, but he neglected to tell me a thing." She frowned in the direction of the bedchamber, clearly wishing she could still berate Lord Wintervale for his shortcomings.

"When was the last time Sir Roderick's ghost was seen?"

"Last night. He was seen walking the labyrinth, clutching the medallion in his hand. The monk who witnessed it was loyal to my husband and came only here. I won't be that lucky next time. You must hurry and get rid of Roderick before the contessa's ball!"

"Where's this labyrinth and what was a priest doing anywhere near it?" Remy asked, imagining a series of caverns with a bull-headed beast at its center.

"The labyrinth." The woman pursed her lips as if she'd bitten into a lemon. "I forget how ignorant the lower classes are. There is a labyrinthine maze painted on the floor of the old chapel beneath the cathedral. The priests and nuns walk it as a form of meditation. I doubt if it's very relaxing with ghosts moaning about."

"Can I see it?" Remy asked, then hastily added, "If I'm to banish this ghost, I'll need to see where he gains access to the realm of the living."

Lady Wintervale's expression grew even more sour. "He came out of the catacombs, obviously."

"Maybe, but if he despises his fate he might avoid returning there. A labyrinth sounds like a likely route into the netherworld, even it is only a painted one."

"I suppose so. I'll have Petru take you in. But don't linger. The monks begin their infernal chants before dawn and I can't risk my man being seen with you."

"Of course." Remy bowed curtly. "I will assess the situation, report to Master Marek, and return with the proper enchantments to send your brother-in-law back to the netherworld."

"He wasn't an entirely bad sort," the lady said with a touch of wistfulness.

"Death often brings out the worst in people," Remy said to console her.

"You don't think Sir Wintervale will come back from the dead, do you?" she asked, showing the first hint of fear.

"Not unless you toss him into the catacombs without a proper burial."

She scowled at him, lifted a tiny silver bill and shook it vigorously. Petru appeared in an instant, and Remy prepared himself for another hike through the rabbit warren that was Wintervale Palace.

5

"Not much to look at, is it?" Remy squinted into the gloom of the cavern. Although a ring of candles on wrought iron stands surrounded the so-called labyrinth, the black lines had faded into the stone floor to such a degree one could walk across it and not realize what it was.

Petru grunted, eyelids drooping. Remy stood at the entrance, a sort of painted keyhole leading one into the spiraling twists and turns of the painted pattern. No monks or ghosts walked the labyrinth this night, but Remy had to admit an aura of menace hung over the place.

Even without a ghost, the underground cavern beneath the cathedral was plenty gloomy, with a low, rough cut ceiling, squat columns that reminded Remy of the enormous weight above his head and hundreds of little niches filled with scowling saints. Remy had never warmed to Christianity, the newly imposed religion of the land, and this place reminded him why. If he had to choose a set of invisible gods to worship, he'd stick to the randy, heavy-drinking gods of the forest, thank you kindly.

A simple black circle indicated the center of the labyrinth. Remy broke through the impulse to walk the pattern, and strode directly across the lines to the center. Petru grunted again, as if he'd never considered such a thing possible.

Remy stopped a few steps shy of the center. He didn't have to stare at it long to confirm his suspicions. The circle was most certainly a portal to another realm. He'd seen enough of them working with Master Marek to recognize the shifty nature of the floor. More often than not portals were how monsters found their way into the world of men. Although perfectly aware of the fact that what he looked at was a dot of paint on a stone floor, it wasn't long before the circle deepened. The paint swirled, creating an ever expanding vortex. The spiral bored deep into the hill, revealing layer upon layer of ruins beneath, and then nothing but hollow darkness.

Low chanting carried through the darkness. Remy tore his gaze from the abyss to see a line of lanterns descending the stairs from the cathedral proper. He cursed and ran to hide behind the nearest pillar. A line of women, all in white, filed into the room, chanting as one. They entered the labyrinth and began circling around it. Remy counted as best he could, though it was hard to keep track as they circled back, crossed paths and intertwined. He guessed thirty was a good number.

In their long gowns they seemed to float, and Remy wondered if they were also ghosts, but they looked too fleshy. Some of them were quite portly, some ruddy, others thin and pale, but all were definitely of the living, even with candles lighting their faces from below and the eerie moaning chant escaping their lips. The strange spectacle continued for what seemed like an hour, until they departed, ascending as they'd descended, chanting all the while. Remy let out the breath he'd been holding. He hadn't moved an inch the entire time.

A hand landed on his shoulder and he nearly leapt out of his skin.

"How dare you defile the chapel with your filthy boots?" A short, stout monk shouted in his ear. "How did you get in here?"

Remy stammered incoherently, looking over the monk's wide shoulders for Petru, but his guide had disappeared. Petru wouldn't risk exposing his lady. Remy had to come up with something quick or he'd end up in the dungeon, where Lady Wintervale would probably poison his gruel in order to keep him quiet.

Praying the man was of a mystical mind, he pointed at the floor. "I came through the labyrinth!"

"Dug a hole through twenty feet of solid stone, did you?" The man clamped down harder. "You're one of them thieves who've been plundering the vaults! I've caught you red-handed. Come along!"

The monk not only couldn't see the portal, he couldn't even imagine it. He dragged Remy out of the labyrinth, shouting for assistance. Remy squirmed but couldn't break free. He was loath to strike a monk, which would only make his situation worse.

Petru had no such qualms. As Remy and his captor passed by one of the thick columns he stepped up behind them and conked the monk on the skull with a stout staff. Remy winced as the man dropped to his knees, grasping the back of his head with two hands.

"Git!" Petru snarled, and vanished into the shadows again. Remy looked around wildly. He was in the heart of forbidden territory and had a long way to go to reach safe ground. Voices and footsteps came from the chapel above. He plunged after Petru, praying his drunken forest spirits wouldn't abandon him in this temple of foreign gods.

He ran straight into something soft and sweet smelling. Something that *oomphed* when he hit it. Winifred Semple.

"This way," she whispered harshly, snatching his hand and dragging him into the shadows.

Remy allowed himself to be led. Even in his panic, he thought of how he'd never touched anything as soft as Winifred's skin. He wondered how soft the rest of her must be and his face blazed. She must have felt his palm burning, heard his heart pounding.

She dragged him up a short, spiraling staircase and into a large open room that smelled of incense and dank stone.

Remy knees locked and he clamped down so hard on Winifred's hand she squeaked.

"What is this place?" he gasped. Moonlight poured in through stained-glass windows and thick columns higher than any tree soared away into darkness.

"The Chapel of Saint Vaclav, silly. Keep moving."

The cathedral. *Of course.* Remy never dreamt he'd set foot in it. Not only was he not a Christian, but not rich, or noble, or in any way worthy of such magnificence. Winifred tugged on his hand.

"It's only an overgrown church," she said.

"I've never been in a church." He moved his feet, but slowly, mind whirling. What would this place look like in sunlight? The inside of the contessa's jewel box?

"Really? Never?"

"What good are they?"

"You're such a pagan," Winifred snapped, but Remy thought he detected the vaguest hint of admiration in her tone. Wishful thinking, for sure.

It got worse. It turned out the chapel they'd emerged in was only an off-shoot of the main building. The thing was enormous. Bigger than the city. Bigger than a mountain.

They ran like mice through a giant's house along an endless center corridor to a heavy side door. Winifred pushed it open and they emerged onto wide steps that led down to the main square.

She pulled up her hood. "Hurry!"

They dashed across the open space to the same staircase Remy and Petru had climbed earlier. Winifred kept going to the first bend, and finally stopped. She faced him and grabbed both his hands.

"You're going to help my lady, aren't you?" she demanded. Lantern light caught copper threads in her hair, and her eyes flashed. "Tell me you're not going to wait around for your master to return."

"This is a tricky business, with a murdering ghost popping up here, there, everywhere. Even in the cathedral." He looked back at the ominous edifice towering over them and shuddered.

"Not in the cathedral. Only down below, in the old parts."

"Is that supposed to make me feel better?"

She put a hand on his cheek and stared straight into his eyes. "I know the real reason Lord Wintervale went to the catacombs. Servants are invisible, you know."

"Not you, Winifred," Remy said, and bit his lip. Was he supposed to call her by name? She didn't seem to care.

"I overheard my lord telling Gavin that he *did* find the medallion on Roderick's corpse. He lied to my lady because she wouldn't approve of him mucking about in the catacombs after treasure. They have plenty of money. It's prestige she's after."

"Treasure?" Remy couldn't fathom what the catacombs had to do with treasure.

"There are carvings on the medallion. They show the way to the tomb hoards of ancient kings. There's not only treasure there, but power. Old power. The power of the people who built the city in the first place. Sir Roderick was trying to conjure it. Maybe he did. Maybe that's why he's back from the dead, killing people. You have to stop him."

"I want to, but—"

"Find it and stop Roderick's ghost." She squeezed his hands and put her face so close to his her breath tickled his ear. "And while you're down there, you might find the treasure yourself. You wouldn't have to tell Lady Wintervale, you know. Finder's keepers."

Remy's palm tingled where her fingers pressed into his skin. He stiffened his spine. "My only concern is to stop the murders."

"Then you're stupid. Gold is all that matters up there." She glared over his shoulder at the cathedral, chin lofted. "What's down below is ours, not theirs. They'd only use it to build more useless towers."

"I see." Remy understood now that Winifred hoped she might charm and cajole him into sharing what he found. He admired such forthright greed. "Is there any-thing more you can tell me about Sir Roderick or how he died?"

"He wasn't a bad sort," she said, mimicking her lady's words. "I think he thought it would be easy, plundering the tombs. You won't make that mistake, will you?"

"Most certainly not."

"Lord Wintervale took the medallion from Roderick's body and went in search of the treasure. He lost his nerve and didn't go far. Maybe his brother's ghost chased him away. I'm sure he stole his bauble back, one way or another. It wasn't among my lord's things. Promise me you won't lose your nerve, even if Roderick moans at you."

"Miss Semple, I'm beginning to think you're more interested in loot than in helping your lady."

"Can't I be interested in both?"

Remy shrugged. "I didn't think a lady would concern herself with robbing dead kings."

Winifred pursed her lips into a pout. "The dead don't care."

"Sometimes they do. Sir Roderick, for instance."

"All the more reason to get rid of him. Promise me you'll do it soon."

"I'll do what I can," Remy said, in spite of his unease. The combination of treasure and a nice smelling girl were too much to resist entirely.

"I know you won't let me down." Winifred squeezed his hand one last time and fled up the stairs. Remy waited a moment before starting down. After a few steps, he realized he had no way contact Winifred or her mistress.

Well, if he failed to banish Sir Roderick's ghost, he was sure he'd be hearing from Lady Wintervale soon enough.

6

THE MESSENGER CROW returned at dawn, drunk and surly.

"Remy the rat boy! Remy the rat boy!" it squawked from its perch on the windowsill. Remy glared at it, bleary eyed and more than little surly himself after a night of no sleep, running from watchmen, dodging the gutter sweepers and, after reaching the safety of home, pouring once more over books that would not give up their secrets.

"Did you find Marek or didn't you, you mite-infested feather brain?"

"Marek is in the Giant Mountains. Giant mountains. Squawk!"

Remy buried his face in his hands. Just his luck to have hired an imbecile of a crow.

"Did you deliver the message?" he asked, jaw tight, palms pressed to his eyes to blot out the weak light.

"Message delivered! Five pence please!"

"I already paid you! Is there a return message?" He'd been disappointed to find no little scroll of paper secured to the crow's leg. Now he'd have to rely on the crow's bird brained remembering of whatever Marek might have said.

"Lost. Quite lost." The crow belched like a sailor. Remy raised his head and the crow bobbed up and down, wings flapping.

"Lost? That's terrible. How could Marek be lost?"

"Fog everywhere. When the fog lifts, I'll be back."

"I can't wait on fog! Lady Wintervale expects me to exorcise her brother-in-law immediately!"

"Wait for me, Remy and don't do anything foolish," the crow said in a perfect rendition of Marek's stern lecturing voice.

"But am I supposed to do nothing while the ghost of Roderick Wintervale murders who knows how many more people? And what about Lady Wintervale, who will surely have me escorted out of the city, never to return, or worse, if I don't help her?"

The crow focused one beady black eye on him. "Nothing foolish."

"But you know nothing about the ghost, the stolen medallion or the haunted labyrinth. Should I send another crow?" Remy rested his chin on his fist, elbow planted in the table. He'd already spent most of the money Marek had left for him to survive on. Besides, if Remy could banish the ghost on his own, the entire fee plus the reward money would be his alone. Except for fifteen percent and the price of a pair of woolen socks he'd promised Glyn, that is.

At least now he knew what he was dealing with. A wronged ghost. A ghost who'd not only been denied a proper burial, but who'd been left in a hole with the common folk. Remy also knew what had to be done. The Wintervales were Christians, so he had to find Roderick's corpse, sprinkle it with holy water, and say the banishing spells he heard Marek chant so often. Of course the best thing to do would be to remove the corpse and inter it in the family vault, but Lady Wintervale had already refused to take the most sensible course.

"Back to the catacombs it is," Remy said.

"Foolish," the crow said and abruptly took flight. Remy sighed. He stood, closed the window, and slid the latch into place. Normally dawn would be the best time to visit the catacombs, but black clouds were blowing in from the north and rain spattered the windowpanes. He'd have little help from the sun today.

He picked up a feather shed by the crow and stuck it in his pocket. Roderick had been dead for over a week. That meant he'd be stowed deeper in the tunnels than Rosie and Abernath. But not too much deeper. This time Remy would take Marek's old staff and dust its tip with oil of mercury, which made a most excellent torch. He'd take Glyn along to carry the trappings of a Christian burial: holy water, a wooden cross, incense, a bible. What else? Best to be thorough.

He began inscribing a list in rough block letters so as not to forget anything. He began to feel better as his plan took shape. With luck, he'd be home and done with the matter in time for lunch.

His hand froze mid-motion as he considered how to prove what he'd done. When Marek banished a monster, he usually had an audience of at least one client. Who would be Remy's audience? No one would believe Glyn, them being mates and all.

"I'll invite the old gang along." His heart warmed to the idea of having his former peers witness his heroic act. They would no longer consider him soft or rat-like, but impressive and confident like Marek. They would all go to the burgomaster to claim his reward, followed by a drunken revelry at the public house. Ursule the barmaid would flirt with him and he would be the hero of the day, maybe even the whole week.

He focused on the idea of Ursule pressing her large breasts against him, but was irritated when the image of Winifred Semple replaced the buxom barmaid. He barked a laugh. Winifred was so far above and beyond Remy the idea was beyond ridiculous, no matter how many lives he saved or monsters he slayed. Even if he brought her the treasure she fancied, she'd never have anything to do with him.

He went outside and waved to a little urchin girl busy prying stones out of the street, probably to sell to the city road repairmen who would use it to patch a hole in a wealthier neighborhood. Remy couldn't help but admire such an enterprising spirit.

"Hey, girl!" he called to her. She sprang to her feet prepared to flee but stopped when he added, "I've got a job for you!"

She stood still, eyeing him warily.

"I'll give you a bun if you go find Glyn and ask him to come here at once."

She wiped her nose on the back of her filthy hand. "Two buns. It's a long way to the wharf. I'll burn off the first just getting there and back."

Remy rolled his eyes. "All right. But hurry."

She fled. That bit of business taken care of, Remy returned to the house. After his celebration party, he would somehow get word of his victory to Lady Wintervale. He paused in front of the shelves of potions, suddenly thoughtful. The stolen medallion had to be worth significantly more than the few coins Lady Wintervale would toss his way. He seriously doubted its worth as a map. Legends of treasure troves were plentiful and yet he'd never met anyone who'd found one. Who needed a whole trove anyway? Could he keep the medallion if he found it?

Remy's head started to ache as he tried to figure out what a spectral being would do with a solid object like a gold medallion. Roderick had been seen clutching it in his ghostly form. It might well be lost to the netherworld, which would be a shame.

He recalled Marek working a spell to call coins up from the bottom of a well, in order to reverse a wish poorly thought out. The coins had landed in Marek's hand, much to Remy's delight, but alas, the wish remained in place and the woman's husband remained stuck in the form of a pig. Marek had not been paid and had to return the recovered coins as well.

But Remy remembered watching Marek mix the potion to attract the gold. Remy remembered everything that had to do with money. He was excitedly mixing potions from memory when Glyn arrived, breathless and rain-sodden.

"The solution is at hand!" Remy announced after admitting his friend.

"Is Marek back?" Glyn asked, craning his neck to look for Marek's black cloak on the hook beside Remy's brown one.

"I've discovered the answer myself," Remy said, his mood dampened. "We must return to the catacombs."

"Oh, joy," Glyn said. "Are you sure?"

"Completely. Cheer up, Glyn, new socks will be yours before the day is out."

Glyn forced a smile, and kept on smiling as Remy related the tale of his adventures the previous night. His smile faded at the news of the unhappy ghost, then regained strength as Remy spoke of the stolen medallion and how it might be his to keep. Glyn grew much brighter when he found out Remy wanted to take the gang along on their adventure. He was nearing a free beer level of cheerfulness when Remy began showing him all the gear he would have to carry in the rucksack, and his happiness plummeted.

At last Remy had gathered everything he thought he needed for a spirit eviction, plus the staff of light, a few extra crystals for Glyn and the gang, and his old stick for bashing in the heads of rats. This he handed to Glyn. He'd never let anyone see him do such menial work again. On a whim, he flipped over a fortune card, and wished he hadn't. The crumbling tower faced him, with dark clouds roiling all around it, lightning striking its turret. Well, he didn't live in a tower, and if one fell, it probably wouldn't have anything to do with him.

They set off down the hill feeling optimistic, with the little urchin at their heels happily munching her second bun. She turned out to be a good crier, and told everyone on the way down how Remy was going to destroy the monster and save the city from ruin.

Most people laughed or catcalled, but some wished him well, and many looked hopeful despite their outward contempt. Soon they'd be throwing roses as his feet and coins in his hat, he thought.

At the wharf Glyn trotted off to round up some of the gang, and Remy descended the narrow stairs to the crumbling quay. Rain fell in thick sheets and the stairs were slick. The river roiled and Remy eyed it with suspicion. It would be most inconvenient if it decided to flood its banks and swamp the catacombs. The vision of swimming through water thick with bones and corpses filled his mind. When he stopped in front of the mouth of the tunnel his confidence faltered.

Dank air blew out and the swirling winds off the river blew in, creating the illusion that the tunnel was breathing. The whistling howl intensified then softened to a moan.

The dead were singing, playing their own bones like chimes.

Remy pulled the bottle of oil of mercury out of the pouch on his belt and dabbed the end of the staff. In the murky daylight it glinted like a new coin. In the tunnels it would give off a soft glow for several hours, plenty of time for Remy to perform his exorcism. Again, onlookers hung over the flood wall and taunted him, but he barely heard them, his mind absorbed with the task at hand.

Why had Roderick Wintervale taken to murdering innocent strangers? What if he were wrong? But that would be too much of a coincidence, with the perpetrator of Roderick's indignity being the first victim. No, it must have been—as was sometimes the case—that after his first kill Roderick's ghost developed a taste for blood.

Death and darkness warped the souls of even the best of men, or so he'd heard. Best to avoid both whenever possible.

Where in the world had Glyn gone to? Did he think Remy wanted to stand around in the rain until thoroughly drenched? He took a step inside the tunnel to move out of the downpour. The glowing staff cast a bright light on the walls, encouraging Remy to move farther in. With the stronger light, the carvings on the walls became clearer. He took a closer look, wishing he really did understand the mysteries of the city's past, as he'd claimed before. There were the carvings of the serpent that he'd seen before at the mouth of the cave, images of battle with men scattered into bits here and there, various monsters, Earendil the vulture who carried the bones of the dead to her nest, and so on.

He reached another, larger depiction of the serpent coiled at the roots of the world tree, and started backward in surprise. The image of the serpent looked exactly like the labyrinth painted on the floor of the chapel thousands of feet above this place.

Remy reflected on this oddity. Had the mythos of the old ones seeped into the consciousness of the last conquerors? Marek said that was often the case. Remy traced the carved labyrinth with his fingertip, shivering at the familiarity of the pattern. Unlike the one in the chapel, this one had many branches in the form of smaller snakes and tree roots that twisted outward from the inner spiral. And in this one, the center wasn't a blank circle but the gaping mouth of the serpent. The chanting nuns wouldn't like this version at all.

"Remy!" Glyn called from what sounded like a long way away. Remy hadn't noticed how far he'd wandered. Obviously his initial childish fear of the darkness was abating, now that he knew what to do.

"Right here!"

Glyn approached, crystal light adding to the glow of Remy's staff. Behind him came Saucy Sadie, Fowler, Ollie Ostrava and a handful of others. Disappointed at the small size of his audience, Remy nonetheless puffed up and greeted them with a stern nod.

"Thank you for joining us on this important civic mission. With your assistance I will banish the ghost that has been murdering our fellow citizens."

"Glyn said there'd be beer," Fowler groused.

"First things first. Has Glyn distributed the light crystals?"

Three of them held up weakly glowing crystals. Not quite as much light as Remy would've liked, but it would have to do.

"Follow me, but stay back."

Remy lead the way and his little troop fell in behind him. His elongated shadow trailed out ahead, cutting an imposing figure across the curved wall. With cloak and staff, his shadow could be mistaken for that of a real alchemist's.

He was a real alchemist, he reminded himself. He just hadn't been given a chance to prove himself. Marek was always guarded with his secrets, and it was in his interest to hold Remy back. After all, if Remy got too adept, he'd be competition. No wonder Marek didn't want to give up control.

Remy's impressive shadow swept across Rosie's corpse. She'd become more compressed over the past day, cheeks hollowed and sunken eyes black as burnt cinders. A thick, rank odor caused bile to rise in his throat. He stopped and looked over his shoulder. His pack glanced around furtively, huddled together.

"The corpse we're looking for was a nobleman. He'll be well dressed, but a bit decomposed."

"What's a nobleman doing down here?" Sadie asked.

"Never mind that. Our job is to get his ghost to leave this realm for good, not gossip about his life story. He died several days ago, so he'll be farther in."

This last bit of information inspired a round of grumbling.

"Glyn said we'd only be down here for a few minutes," Fowler said, and Sadie nodded. They seemed to be banding together against him. Remy was tempted to tell them to leave, but he needed them. No, didn't *need* them, but preferred to have their warmth and light as backup, just in case.

"It can't be much farther. There haven't been that many bodies tossed in here over the past week." Remy set an example by striding forward confidently, and almost immediately cracked his head on the ceiling, which was getting lower and craggier the deeper in they went.

Fowler guffawed, Sadie giggled, and Remy cursed. Rubbing his head, he continued on, holding his staff out ahead to light the way. The corpses they could see now were more deteriorated: skin desiccated, lips drawn back, hints of greenish decay around their extremities. And there were more bones, probably exhumed by the retreating river tides last spring. Tumbled bodies lay in tangled knots, eddies of half-rotting flesh and exposed bone.

Remy fought his natural instinct to look away and pointed his staff at every fresh looking pile of corpses. Although the air grew colder, he started to sweat, skin clammy and heart beat swift. His chest cramped and he realized he was holding his breath, not wanting to breathe in too much of the rot heavy in the air. Here and there he spotted more of the serpent spirals on the walls, twisting and entangling, growing more and more elaborate, less like the neat meditation path in the cathedral, more like a true maze of diabolical construction.

At this point he reached a fork in the tunnel. He should've brought old Silas with him, but the grave man would've overcharged for his services. It shouldn't be this hard to find a dead man. How far could he have gone?

"Which way?" Glyn whispered over his shoulder.

"His brother must have taken him in this far to hide his shameful act." He swept his staff over the ground, looking for signs of disturbance. He didn't see any, but went with his gut. "This way," he said, and followed the tunnel to the right.

They'd reached a place where there was no ambient light, no slight trickle of illumination from the city outside. Blackness chewed at the edges of their tiny pools of light. Water dripped from the ceiling, plunking on stone, seeping through his thin cloak. He wouldn't take them much farther, and they wouldn't follow even if he tried. Disappointment formed a lump in his belly as he faced the prospect of failure.

"That man looks fancy," Glyn commented. Remy stopped to look into the crevice Glyn illuminated with his crystal. The corpse in question stood almost upright, having been wedged into a crack in the wall. Other arms and legs stuck out around him. One ghoulish face leered over his shoulder, but Roderick, if this was indeed him, looked fairly reposed. His eyes were closed, stringy hair clinging like tendrils to waxy skin, but having started out with more flesh on his bones than most of the corpses down here, he hadn't become ghastly yet. Not that he looked well.

"That must be him." Remy approached and inspected the luxurious black velvet coat, leather pants and ruffled silk shirt. Roderick too was without shoes, his long toes encased in white silk socks.

"Must've done some horrible crime to end up down here," Fowler said. The others whispered to each other, spinning a story to account for the fancy man's presence in this hole to the netherworld. Just as well. Their gossiping might help cover up his real identity, something for which Lady Wintervale would be grateful. Maybe she'd call on Remy again for her alchemy needs. Maybe she'd send the sweet-smelling Winifred to fetch him.

The sense memory of white lilacs combined with the rot thick in the air nearly made him gag. Obviously now was not the time for romantic fantasies.

"Hand me the sack," he said to Glyn. Glyn shrugged off his load and held out his crystal to help Remy search through the contents. He handed the cross to Fowler, the bible to Sadie, who took it with a shudder like he'd handed her a wet rat, and the incense burner to Ollie. Remy lit a white candle and used it to ignite the incense. Again, the rich scent of Myrrh struck Remy as sickening in this dank atmosphere, but it would help to repel the spirits of the dead as well as normal folk.

Remy braced himself and reached out to search Roderick for the medallion. With the slight shifting of his jacket, Roderick slumped and the arms of the dead behind him flailed, seeming to grasp for Remy. He jumped back, expecting the corpses to all come tumbling forward, but they didn't.

Fowler chuckled, but it was a nervous, scratchy sound. Ollie emitted a low whine.

Remy continued his search, but found nothing. He wasn't surprised. If Roderick's spirit could transport the blasted thing, why would he trust it to his fleshy remains? Roderick must have it with him in his ghostly form. So the question presented itself—should Remy cast the spell for drawing up gold first, or the banishing spell? If he banished Roderick before securing the medallion, it would surely be lost forever.

"What are you dilly dallying about for?" Fowler exclaimed.

"It's a delicate matter. I'm searching for any cursed talismans that might be binding his spirit to his corpse."

Remy made up his mind. He would call up the gold first, and if Roderick showed up along with it, Remy would have the holy water ready. Simple.

He handed his staff to Glyn and removed the vial holding the coin-attracting potion from his cloak. He sprinkled a bit on Roderick as he chanted the words of the spell.

A silvery mist formed and seeped out from around the wedged-in bodies. Remy took heart. Something was happening, anyway. His audience shuffled backward, but

Remy stood firm. He'd need to be ready to snatch the medallion the instant it appeared.

A loud groan came from deep in the tunnel and the crevice holding Roderick upright widened with a resounding crack.

"Quake!" Sadie screeched and bolted along with most of the others. Glyn, Fowler and Ollie remained rooted to the spot. They weren't going to run if Remy didn't.

"It's only an illusion," he assured them, voice quivering a little. "The pits of hell are opening and our ghost will be here soon. Nothing to worry about."

The bodies behind Roderick tumbled back to the floor, but he remained upright. Remy could now see that the crevice had no visible end. It stretched away into utter blackness, except for the mist, which sparkled, revealing flecks of gold, silver and gemstones imbedded in the walls.

Remy gaped in surprise. He didn't see the medallion, but the treasure in the crevice far exceeded the worth of one little bauble. They remained fixed in the walls however, and Remy felt their pull. His spell wasn't strong enough to pry them free. Roderick continued to stand in his way.

"All right then. Step two." He put away the gold attracting potion and removed the holy water. "Any one know any Christian prayers?"

Ollie began to chant in Latin. When he noticed everyone staring at him in surprise, he stopped. "I was raised by the sisters in the village church 'til I was five," he explained. "Then the king burned down the church and beheaded the sisters. Damn shame if you ask me." He cleared his throat and began chanting again. The foreign words made it sound impressive.

Remy turned back to Roderick, called out his banishing spell, and splashed holy water in Roderick's face. Nothing happened. The mist continued to lick at Remy's ankles and he shivered. He was growing less concerned with summoning the ghost and more concerned with moving the rigid corpse to get at the treasure beyond. He repeated the spell, louder, fairly dousing Roderick's head with holy water. The man remained unimpressed.

"Ox balls," Remy muttered and pushed against Roderick's chest. He didn't budge. Remy tried to squeeze by, but the opening was too tight.

"Are you sure that's a good idea?" Glyn asked, voice tremulous.

"Of course it's—"

Roderick's eyes opened, inches from Remy's. Remy quickly reconsidered his greed. The eye sockets of the corpse contained no fleshy eyeballs, only small wriggling snakes that spilled out and slithered down his face, neck, and shoulders. Remy tried to leap back but Roderick's frozen hand clamped onto his forearm, preventing his escape.

"*Rafar Ramari Eltoo*! Be gone, dead man. You do not belong here!" Remy cried and emptied the vial into Roderick's face. His flesh sizzled but he was not deterred.

The mist darkened, roiled and began to breathe, a metal-on-metal rasp that hurt Remy's ears. The bite of hot tar stung his eyes as the thing solidified into a black ooze seeping out of the crevice. It grew outstretched arms ending in hooked claws. This was the real monster. The monster that killed.

"Run!" he shouted. The shadow beast took on sharp angles and thrust out around the corpse like blades. The tip of one pierced Glyn's chest, pinning him to the tunnel wall. A grimace of terror peeled Glyn's lips back and stuck there. The staff he held fell to the floor with a clatter, his fingers raised and hooked in a defensive posture.

Fowler and Ollie screamed as one and fled. Remy couldn't blame them, even though the shadow beast vanished in an instant, apparently satisfied with its act of violence. He would've run too, if he could.

"Glyn!" he cried, but his friend was frozen stiff, his skin deathly white in the weird, vicious light pouring forth from the mouth of hell. Remy could spare him no time, for he now wrestled with Roderick's corpse for his own life.

He chanted the spell over and over. Roderick's black mouth gaped at him, full of broken, jagged teeth, but he didn't move. The floor of the crevice opened and bodies began to spill into the crack. Remy jerked and strained against the grip on his arm but couldn't break free.

"Curse you, Roderick Wintervale! Return to hell and stay there! Now!" Remy punched the corpse in the chest as hard as he could and Roderick began to topple backward.

Unfortunately, he did not release his grip. Remy struggled wildly against the dead man's vice-like grip, straining to keep his feet in the tunnel as Roderick dragged him toward the crevice. His boots slid along the wet stone. He grasped at the sides of the crevice but could find no purchase.

One last jerk and he freed himself, but it was too late. He'd lost his balance and couldn't recover. He and Roderick plummeted into the abyss. The gleaming jewels winked out and Remy plunged into utter darkness with a rain of corpses falling around him. He curled into a tight ball, preparing for impact.

7

REMY FELL LONGER than he ever wanted to think about or contemplate again. He fell long enough for the sick lurching feeling in his chest to claw along his spine and release out of his mouth in a hollow screech he barely recognized as his own. He fell long enough to relive his short, worthless life and to contemplate a long, painful death.

A minute? Half a minute? Whatever length it was, it must have been much shorter than he thought. As corpses slapped and spattered beneath him, he quickly whispered a blow-blocking spell. When he hit a yielding mound of irregular consistency, the blow forced out all his air but didn't kill him.

He sucked rank, sticky air into his resisting lungs, trying not to think of the miasma crawling into his throat, poisoning his guts with the stench of death. But he had to breathe, didn't he? He was still alive. His back ached from the impact, radiating outward in waves of pain.

Finally he drew in enough air to be able to think.

He opened his eyes to nothing. Not a scrap or wink or glint of light reached him. He sensed a great open chasm around him by the sound of water dripping far away. Beneath the drips were more noises. Wind, perhaps, which gave him hope of some unseen exit. But as his hearing sharpened he recognized the sound as slithering. The hiss and rasp of scales across … Remy sat up, ignoring fresh stabs of pain.

Cautiously he reached down and poked at the ground with a finger. It gave way into a moist, fleshy consistency. Because it was flesh. Remy recoiled.

He sat upon a mound of corpses. His skin crawled and every last hair stood on end. He tried to struggle to his feet but the bodies gave way and he sank ankle deep into a mess of bone, cloth and fluid. He pushed with his hands and felt a skull, still a bit fleshy, partially wrapped in a piece of damp velvet.

He regained his feet and moved as quickly as he could across the pile, hoping to reach its end somewhere in the blackness. The slithering of snakes was joined by gulping noises, the clacking of fang against bone, the slobber of flesh ground down to a pulp.

"Dear Goddess, God, anyone who can hear! Please save me!" Remy cried. He was in danger of losing his mind as he flailed and thrashed against this open pit of death. If only he could fly. If only he had his staff.

He thought of Glyn pierced by the strange monster and his despair increased. If not for the sickening reality of his circumstance, he might have fallen into a heap to die. But lying down was not an option.

He plowed onward until at last he reached a place where the mound sloped down and he stumbled the last several steps to a raw stone wall.

"Thanks to all that is light, clean, and pure," Remy whispered, clinging to the wall as if salvation were just beyond it. He wiped the gunk from his hands against the rough stone and paused to consider.

He'd fallen into the deepest pit of the catacombs, that much was obvious. These were man-carved caverns, and so there must be a way out. If he didn't panic, or stopped panicking, anyway, he would find his way out. He was, after all, an alchemist.

An alchemist who fell prey to his own spells, allowing the gold spell to pull him down instead of rising to him. Banishing himself along with the spirit he'd conjured. Calling up a strange mist that killed his best friend.

The thought of Glyn's death paralyzed Remy. He deserved to die down here. He'd been cast into hell for a reason. He banged his forehead against the stone. The pain helped just a little.

What helped more was a sudden loud hiss behind him. He turned and was greeted by his first glimpse of light.

The eyes of the flesh-eating serpent glowed crimson, but did not illuminate its surroundings.

Two ruby slits focused on Remy and that was all he needed to set himself into motion. He slid as quickly as he could along the wall, stumbling over limbs and bones. The eyes tracked him. Remy imagined a snake might enjoy hunting something that moved for once, or maybe it was too fat and lazy to give much of a chase.

But the eyes kept coming and soon they were everywhere Remy looked, burned into his light-starved corneas.

"Light! Light!" Remy chanted. At last he remembered the oil of mercury in his pocket. But what to use as a torch? He crouched down and felt through the rotting corpses. Here at the lower end of the mound there was less flesh, more bone and his fingers eventually wrapped around a clean length of bone, maybe an arm or leg. He rubbed the knobby tip clean and dabbed it with a bit of oil.

It flared, stabbing into his eyes so he was even blinder than before. He looked away, eyes open to slits. When his vision began to creep back, he almost wished it hadn't.

Coiled upon the horror of the corpse mound was a white snake. Longer than a horse and cart, fatter than a wine barrel, it wove its thick body in and out of the bones. Its red eyes narrowed. It didn't like the light, but it wasn't afraid.

Remy flailed the bone in his hand back and forth and the snake tracked it, head whipping side to side. Remy thought he might throw it to distract the monster, but he dare not waste a dab of the mercury oil.

He waved the light around and thought he detected a tunnel mouth many yards away around the curving chamber.

"Shoo!" he shouted at the snake. The snake flicked a forked tongue at him but didn't move. Remy made for the tunnel and the snake didn't follow. The relief was so profound he nearly burst into tears.

"Steady on, Remy," he said to himself in his best Marek voice. "If you're going to fall apart, do so after you've escaped the immediate danger."

He kept moving, knees wobbling, breath ragged. When he reached the dark spot he was once again relieved beyond words to find it really was a tunnel, not just a smear of shadow. His elation was somewhat dampened to see a set of stairs leading down, not up.

He turned to flash his light around the cavern and was startled to see the snake very close behind him. Beyond this fearsome image the corpse mound rose higher than a two-story mansion and above it, a blackness with no end.

"Down it is," Remy muttered, and slipped into the tunnel.

Narrow steps worn concave in the center by centuries of footsteps led straight downward, with no turns or landings to break the descent. The tunnel was narrow enough Remy could rub his elbows along each wall if he kept his arms bent. Instead he trailed a palm along one side and held the glowing bone before him. The bottom of the stairs, if there was one, wasn't visible. The black, enclosed space tightened in on Remy and his steps faltered. His calves tightened, and as the steps grew even steeper, vertigo assailed him. There was barely room for his entire boot on the steps. If he slipped, he'd tumble into the unknown.

But what could be worse than a mountain of rotting corpses? Remy shivered. He most certainly did not want to find out. Just as he was about to drop from exhaustion, he reached a flat bit of floor and collapsed on to it.

He stretched out briefly, resting his aching legs and back before sitting up. A few steps ahead the staircase once again led downward. To either side, a tunnel led out along more or less even ground, curving almost immediately so that what lay beyond wasn't visible.

Did it matter which way he went? Was this a life and death decision? Left, to more corpses and digestion in the belly of snake? Right, to light, fresh air and sweet, sweet life? Forward and down? Back and up? The last sounded the least appealing.

The glow of his bone torch was fading, but he decided to wait until it faded entirely to refresh it. He only had the small bottle of oil, and that half full. If he ran out of light, he was doomed for sure. Not that he wasn't doomed for sure already, but at least light created the illusion of hope.

He sighed heavily. He couldn't even take a scrap of comfort from knowing he'd rid the city of Roderick's ghost. The murderer wasn't a ghost at all, but that thing in the crevice. Maybe with the opening of the abyss the monster had fallen in too. The murders would end and the wharf dwellers would make up songs about him. He'd die a hero, but without ever having the chance to enjoy it.

And if the monster had fallen in, was it close behind him? Tracking him? Was this where it lived when it wasn't murdering?

A wheeze followed by a cough brought him to an upright position. He looked around wildly, but saw nothing. It must have been the odd snuffling breeze that coursed through the tunnels. Then something rustled and Remy clambered to his feet.

"Who goes there?" he shouted. His voice trailed off in four directions; up, down, right, left. A moment later it returned in four loud echoes, each slightly slower than the last. They repeated in a fading roundelay until all became quiet once again.

Did all of the tunnels spiral around and return to this spot? Remy sagged under renewed despair.

"Clever beast you are," a rough voice said. Remy spun around to face the stairs he'd just descended.

Roderick Wintervale stood in the narrow passage, looking as dead as ever. Red scorch marks blemished his face where Remy had thrown holy water on him, but otherwise he appeared unchanged.

"Clever?" Remy asked. That was the last word he'd ever use to describe his recent activities.

"It's not easy for a living man to gain entrance to the labyrinth. My brother failed after a rather feeble attempt. I feel, however, it was quite rude of you to try to cast me into hell just so you could raid its hidden treasures."

Remy nearly laughed. The idea that he would have entered this stinking pit on purpose was ridiculous.

"I cast you into hell to stop you from murdering people," he said. He wasn't quite ready to admit the rest had been a horrible mistake.

"I never murdered anyone. Not even my miserable brother." Roderick descended the last couple stairs, footsteps hushed as his silk socks brushed against the stone. "All I ever did was steal this." He lifted his hand and held out a gleaming gold medallion.

All of Remy's treasure lust had been sapped out of him, but as he looked at the gold disc, something about it caught his eye. It was engraved with a spiral. A labyrinth. Was that the map Winifred spoke of?

"What was that beast?" he asked.

"If you wander these passageways long enough you'll surely find out. Hot pulsing blood attracts the worst kind of ghouls."

"You've been seen in the cathedral, Sir Roderick. Can you show me the way out?"

"Why would I do that? You cursed me to hell!"

"I apologize for my error. Please help me, and I'll make sure your remains are returned to the family vault." Remy had no idea how he'd do that, but he'd move mountains to get out of this place.

Roderick laughed, exposing his rows of broken teeth. Thankfully in this form he wasn't infested with snakes.

"My dear sister-in-law will make sure that never happens. She's the one who had me killed and convinced my brother to toss my bones into the catacombs."

"Whatever for?"

"A sacrifice." Roderick gazed at the floor. "That is why I walk the labyrinth. To cleanse my soul of the dark curse attached to my death." He lifted the medallion and traced a ghostly finger along its spirals.

"A sacrifice? To what end?" Remy recast his conversation with Lady Wintervale in this new light. She wasn't afraid of scandal. She was afraid of her victim's revenge. Afraid Sir Roderick would find his way out of the catacombs to haunt and confound her.

"There is no end. Only spiral upon spiral. The serpent eating its own tail and so on." Roderick shook himself from his reverie and looked up at Remy, hollow eyes smoldering. "You may be clever, but you're also mad. Tell me, alchemist, what good is treasure if you don't know the way out?"

"I didn't come here for treasure. I came to stop the murders!"

"I don't believe you. And even if I did, you can't walk through stone, can you?" Roderick walked past Remy and straight into the wall, vanishing with a laugh.

Remy blinked at the space where he'd been. It was entirely possible he'd hallucinated the visitation. He was dead tired. The weight of the city pressed down on him from above and the horrors of hell licked at the ground beneath his feet. His bone torch grew faint. He needed to rest, if he could, as impossible as that sounded.

He found a place against a flat bit of wall and sat, knees pulled up, cloak tight around him, bone clutched in one fist. If the ghost were real, and what he said was true, Remy needed to contemplate what it all meant. Murder. Human sacrifice. The labyrinth above and the maze below. He rested his forehead on his knees and sank into an uneasy sleep.

8

THE SCENT OF WHITE LILACS invaded Remy's monster-infested dreams, a soothing tentacle arising from a world that existed only in the deepest recesses of his mind, in the form of a scrap or two of memory. Bread baking. The chopping of wood for a snapping hearth fire. A half-sung, half-murmured lullaby. The sensation of being held and rocked. A hand on his shoulder, soft at first, then harder, claws digging into his skin, shaking him.

He awoke with a start to total blackness. He flailed at his shoulder but there was nothing there, no one grasping him. Sharp tingles of pain lanced outward from his neck and he realized the lingering affects of his fall must have conjured the sensation of claws digging into his flesh.

He took slow, calming breaths as he tried to orient himself. Colors flashed on the walls and swam away, but they existed only in his mind. There was no light and therefore no color. He felt around for the bone, which he'd let go of in his sleep. Panic raced through him when his hand didn't immediately land on it, but he found it after a moment's scrabbling and grasped it tight, fingers aching from having clutched it for so long.

He carefully dabbed a bit of oil of mercury on it and sighed with relief as the end of the bone began to glow once more. His relief was short lived as his circumstances crowded in on him. The same four passageways awaited his decision.

Clambering to his feet with the wall for support, he stretched out his aching limbs, shuddered off the cold damp, and found a spot to relieve himself. His throat was parched, but not enough to lick the walls for whatever moisture they might provide. That might come soon enough.

Aside from not going up to the serpent's lair, or down, there was really nothing to recommend one tunnel over the other. He took a knee and fumbled in his pockets for whatever magical bits and bobs he'd thought to bring. On the floor he spread out his armament: three entirely unmagical pennies, a small knife with a bone handle and leather sheath used for the occasionally necessary letting of blood, a folded scrap of paper on which he'd written out the spells that had backfired so horribly, a crow's feather, a small pouch of herbs, a tin of powdered copper, a handful of beads and a votive candle he'd snitched from the cathedral.

The candle and the knife were great boons. The worth of everything else was up to chance. And not a scrap to eat or drink. His gut churned as he thought of the two buns he'd given the urchin.

Clearing his throat, he announced to the darkness, "I'll find my way out today and take these three pennies straight to the public house for a beer and bun." He pocketed them and then reconsidered. When they'd been lost before, Marek had flipped a coin to choose a direction. Not one to leave things to chance, he'd muttered a spell of guidance. Remy remembered a few words and thought he might lace the rest of the spell together from what he knew of charm crafting.

"That hasn't worked so well for you," he said, but now was not the time to question his one skill. Yes, his knowledge was imperfect, but he couldn't give up on alchemy altogether.

He pulled out a penny. On one side was the profile of some dead king, on the other an image of the old fortress in the center of the castle. Remy warmed the coin in his hand, closing his eyes and envisioning Marek's cozy hovel with its thick walls, crackling hearth and well-stocked pantry.

"King left. Tower right." Whispering the half-remembered words of the guiding spell, he tossed the coin in the air. The coin bounced, spun, and landed tower up.

With an unhappy quiver he recalled the image from the fortune telling card he'd idly flipped before leaving on his adventure: the crumbling tower.

But it was never a good idea to second-guess a coin toss, especially one guided by an enchantment. He picked up the coin and the rest of his bits and bobs, then stood and gazed down the tunnel to his right. Naturally the tunnel to the left suddenly appeared more appealing, for no reason other than a contrary mind.

Before he could drive himself mad with indecision he strode into the tunnel to his right. It curved left and sloped upward ever so slightly, inspiring a wave of unreasonable optimism to flood through him.

"Why, after all, would the ancient peoples have built an endless series of tunnels to nowhere? Surely they didn't have that much time and labor to waste."

The pit that had become the lair of bones and serpents had probably once been a great hall or temple. All these tunnels must have been service corridors that led to kitchens and sleeping chambers and whatnot.

"Odd folk, these old ones," he murmured. Trying to calculate how far beneath the city he was, he imagined a great upside down city, spreading down into the earth instead of up to the sky. He supposed back when there were still giants and gods mucking about, an underground city might have seemed like a good idea.

"Am I the first living soul in a thousand years to wander these halls? Why, I might just write a history of the old ones when I return, being a first-hand expert and all. Not even Marek knows about this place."

Remy filled his mind with pleasant thoughts of standing in a fancy room like the one Lady Wintervale greeted him in, holding forth on the spectacular nature of the ruins beneath their feet. Scholars would scribble rapid notes and ladies would gaze upon him in admiration. Marek, giving grudging respect at first, would at last concede that his pupil had out paced him in stature, which was only right. Remy would be generous with his new found wealth.

The tunnel forked and he paused. This time the decision was easy because one branch sloped downward while the other continued up. Remy's optimism grew. He'd be at the river in no time. He'd managed to distract himself for several minutes and wondered what new fantasy he could spin when something on the floor drew his attention. He crouched down and brushed away bits of rubble and dirt. His fingers found the grooves of a labyrinth before his eyes did.

He lowered his bone torch, excited to think the carving might be some sort of map, or offer a clue of some kind. The design was rough, large and infinitely complex. Remy's eyes hurt trying to make out all the interlocking spirals. He dearly hoped this was not an accurate representation of the tunnels. What would be the point of so vast a maze? To hide a great treasure? To imprison a monster, like in the tales he heard from the southern lands?

"It's just art, and therefore meaningless," Remy said. Still he stared at the thing. The old ones were clearly obsessed with the image. One decorated Roderick's medallion. Remy's mind went blank, then lurched slowly into motion.

What had Lady Wintervale unleashed with her sacrifice? Could he believe a battered ghost over a finely dressed lady? Was the monster still on the loose, freed from the pits of hell by an old lady? For what purpose?

"Money." Remy nodded to himself. Money was the purpose behind everything. Winifred was right about that. And the more money one had, the crazier one became for it, or so it seemed. The vision he'd had of the jewel-encrusted tunnels had probably been true, and Lady Wintervale knew it. She'd sacrificed her brother-in-law, who she must not have liked very much, in order to open a way into the labyrinth. In doing so, she'd freed one of its many monsters.

Feeling fairly confident in his conclusions, Remy reconsidered his proposed treatise on the nature of the tunnels. If—when—he escaped the darkness, he should really keep things to himself. He could return better prepared in order to seek the treasure. Maybe he could wrest the medallion from Roderick's ghostly fingers. Maybe he'd let Marek help, if his former boss promised not to be too bossy. They could be partners. Fifty-fifty.

"Glyn was your partner. Glyn died for the promise of fifteen percent and a pair of socks." Remy scowled. Before he could seek treasure, he had to solve the case of the murdering monster and banish the correct demon to hell. Then he could give in to greed and stupidity once again.

"Are you sure that's a good idea?" he asked, mimicking his friend's constant doubt. He smiled weakly. "No, Glyn. I am sure of nothing."

He returned his attention to the carving on the floor and noticed an X notched into a groove, right in front of a place where the groove split in two.

"Is that where I am?" The groove to the right led off into a dizzying series of spirals and branches. The groove to the left curved for a while before ending abruptly, cut through with a slash mark.

"But left leads up!" he whined. He stared into the maw of each tunnel. All of his instincts resisted going down, which was where the tunnel to the right clearly led. "This might not even be accurate." He waved his hand over the carving. The X's and slashes might be accidental scuffs added over the centuries. There was nothing convincingly deliberate about them. Was that really an X, or just a couple of scratches? He wiped away more dirt and held the bone torch closer, but couldn't convince himself one way or the other.

"I'm not going down," he said and stood. He took a deep breath and for one tantalizing instant thought he smelled the mineral and garbage stench of the river. "Upward!" he cried, and plunged into the tunnel to his left.

It grew steeper as it curved and suddenly there were stairs, leading straight up into darkness. Remy's heart leapt. The way out! The carving had probably been a trick. Some ancient trickster or monster didn't want anyone to get out.

He climbed quickly at first, slowing as his lungs began to protest. This was much steeper than the climb to the castle from the old quarter. Straight up, no zigs or zags or landings. Remy wasn't about to complain, even if there'd been anyone around to complain to. Instead he hummed, a sort of breathless wheeze, to prove to the darkness he was no longer afraid. Yes, he'd hit a rough patch, what with Glyn's death, the rotting corpses, the flesh-eating serpents and the absolute darkness, but he'd be free soon.

His hum vibrated up and down the tunnel, reverberating against the stone, intensifying and fading. An answering whistle came. Wind through a crevice? The whistle deepened into a low screech, grating like knives clashing in close combat. Was it the monster, following him up the stairs? Remy dearly hoped not.

The screech ended in what sounded suspiciously like a snort. Remy paused, listening intently. Nothing but the constant drip, drip, drip. He caught his breath and continued. A fire burned in his lungs, but he kept moving. Now he was sure he was regaining all the ground he'd lost in his plummet and the journey down the stairs. Even if his heart burst he wouldn't stop. Nothing would stop him. Nothing.

He stopped. Gasping, he leaned against the wall.

"When will this end?" he cried. Again, his voice flew up and down, expanding, turning back on itself, stirring up the wind, the moans and groans of the tunnels, all picking up his cry. When—will—this—end?

His cry sank away into drip, drip, drip. The stones grumbled. Or was it his stomach? Now he was agonizingly thirsty. When he reached the river he'd jump in and gulp the oily water until he exploded. At least his exertion had beaten back the cold. Sweat slicked his face, skin flushed with heat.

He looked up. Where before he'd only seen a pinpoint of blackness, he now detected a faraway glint. Sunlight?

"Thank the Goddess, the old gods, even the murdered son of the Christian father," he wheezed. "I will visit every temple in the land and make an offering if only I can see the sun again."

Placing one foot in front of the other, he climbed, head down, not daring to look again for fear it had been a trick of his bone torch reflecting off a mineral vein, a pocket of gold, a gemstone squeezed out of the earth. How worthless those things were in comparison to a ray of sunlight. At this very moment, the sun fell freely upon the faces of all those lucky enough not to have fallen into a pit of corpses and vipers.

The next time Remy looked, he saw a door at the top of the stairs. His light reflecting off the metal bolt mechanism had caused the glint.

Pulse pounding in his ears, he climbed faster, ignoring the pain in his thighs. A small landing, maybe three times the width of single stair, jutted out from the very solid looking door. Remy stumbled against it, cheek pressed to the wood, chest heaving.

"Please open," he rasped, grabbing the pull and tugging. The bolt didn't budge. He chuckled softly. Of course it wouldn't be that easy. He crouched down to examine the keyhole.

The lock was simple, but it most likely hadn't budged in years, centuries. A lock frozen with rust. He peeked through the hole and as expected saw nothing but blackness. At least no red eye peered back at him.

He knelt on the landing and removed the tin of powdered copper. A basic ingredient in many alchemical potions, the copper combined with a bit of heat could eat away at the rust. He would light the candle with a dab of mercury and heat the powder on the blade of his dagger, which would also serve as a pick! With everything coming together so splendidly he couldn't help but worry.

What lay on the other side of the door? Once he had the candle lit he paused to listen to the constant dripping, the scraping wind, his heart pounding. For an abandoned, buried ruin, the pit was an awfully noisy place, especially when he was trying to sift out natural sounds from the clack of claws on stone, or the strained breathing of subterranean nightmares lurching about in the shadows.

"Stop it," he whispered, though his hands shook as he sprinkled powder on the blade. "Aside from Roderick and those snakes, this place is as barren as the king's heart."

The white candle, smelling slightly of beeswax and vanilla, cheered him immensely. Nothing could harm him while he basked in its glow.

The copper powder began to crackle and he swiftly inserted the blade in the keyhole, tapping out the powder into the mechanism while reciting a spell for undoing knots. The sharp bite of the smoke curled into his nostrils and he sneezed.

A moment later an answering sneeze came from the other side of the door.

"Echo," Remy said. He proceeded to work the lock. For this he needed no alchemy, having been a master picklock during his years on the streets. The bar holding the bolt in place was large and his blade thin. He worked carefully to avoid snapping it against the iron. His palms grew sweaty. A splinter worked its way into his cheek where he pressed his face to the door. The click and scrape of his blade returned to him in a series of scratchy echoes, as if an army of spiders were creeping up the stairs, coming for him.

With a loud clank, the bar gave way. Gasping thanks, he lifted the pull once more and tugged the bolt aside. It moved reluctantly, and loudly, emitting a hideous screech. The door opened with a creak to wake the dead.

After refreshing his torch, he blew out the candle. He gathered his things and tucked them away, but kept the knife in his hand. Shoulder to the door, he pushed against it. The hinges wailed, announcing his presence to all and sundry.

Belatedly, he thought to shift his knife to his fighting hand and the torch to the other. He'd been clinging to the bone for so long it felt like an extension of his own arm. He held it up and wondered who it had belonged to.

Beyond the white bone in his upraised hand there seemed to be more bones floating in blackness. He blinked and shook his head. The dark was playing tricks again. A row of white columns led away into the shadows. He swept the bone back and forth and saw that he was in a large chamber ringed with columns. They were roughly carved, no art to them and they supported a raw stone ceiling, but this change in architecture fueled Remy's optimism. Out of the pit, into the ... temple?

In the center of the large room sat a round object, an altar or perhaps the foundation of a missing column. He moved cautiously toward it, noting as he walked the grooved indentations on the floor.

Another damn labyrinth spiraled around the entire area of the floor.

"Apparently these people had nothing better to do," he mused. Of course, if one lived in a maze, one might be well advised to memorize its twists and turns. Remy thought about all the labyrinthine images he'd seen and realized they'd all been different. "Doesn't seem helpful."

He stopped at the circular object, which was about as high as his hips. It was a well, with a thick rim all around it. Extending his torch over it, he could see that an iron framework had once blocked it, but the iron bars had been twisted and pulled asunder. The distant sound of water lapping far below fired his thirst, but he had no interest whatsoever in exploring another pit.

He backed away, into the freezing arms of a dead man.

"Ready to fly again?" Roderick cackled in his ear, propelling Remy rapidly forward. Remy braced himself against the edge of the well and swung his torch around like a club. The bone sailed clean through the ghost. Roderick's image tore like a flag in a storm.

Remy wrenched free of the ghostly hand on his arm and ran, stopping only when he reached a column. He clung to it, cursing over his shoulder. "Why won't you stay in hell where you belong?"

Roderick sniffed, watching with a pained expression as the tear in his chest mended. "I was only having a bit of fun."

Keeping the bulk of the column between them, Remy glared at him. "Now I know why Lady Wintervale had you murdered!"

"Oh, come now. Don't you want to find the treasure?" Roderick asked, his expression wounded.

"No! I want out."

"Whatever for? What's out that isn't in? Out is only a pale a reflection of in. A trick of light. Only in pure darkness can you see what is real."

"You've been down here too long, Sir Roderick. Have you forgotten about sunrise, and flowers, and … beer?"

"Oh, no. I will never forget about beer." Roderick's broken mouth stretched into a grimace. "But you will, once you seize the treasure. All you have to do is reach the bottom and this is the quickest way down." He pointed into the well. Remy shuddered.

"Is there a bottom?"

Roderick shrugged. "Is there a top to the sky?"

Remy sighed. There was no reasoning with ghosts. "Why do you care what I do?"

"You're my only hope, Remy the rat boy." Roderick shook his head. "If only I were still alive so I could slit my wrists."

"Hope for what?"

"To stop my murderer from getting what she wants."

"What does Lady Wintervale want?"

"What does any power-hungry whore of a witch want?" Roderick shouted the question, waving his arms in agitation. The columns groaned in response.

"Treasure?"

"The throne, you fool! Ultimate power."

"But the king is alive. Fat and healthy by all accounts."

"Not for long." Roderick began to pace, trailing threads of grey mist behind him. "She will unlock the labyrinth and unleash its horrors on the world above. Light will be consumed by eternal night."

"That sounds a bit extreme." Remy wondered if death had driven Roderick mad.

"She doesn't understand. No one understands who hasn't roamed these tunnels. You, Remy, you understand now." Roderick pointed a ghostly finger at him.

"Yes, I do. So it only makes sense that you should help me escape, so that I can warn the king. Summon the army. Raise the alarm and so on."

"No one will listen to you, Remy the rat boy. Do you think you might gain audience with the king? No, you must stop her. You must go down."

"I'm not jumping into any hole!"

"But you did before. And this hole is smaller, its monsters long ago escaped."

"That was an accident!"

"There are no accidents in the labyrinth. Only bad choices." Cocking his head to the side, Roderick smiled, the slightest trace of his formerly handsome face flashing across his ghoulish features. "And their consequences," he said, and dove head first into the well.

"Damn ghost," Remy muttered. But then he heard what must have sent Roderick over the edge. A rumble that was not of stone but of flesh, a groan from the belly of some vast beast, made the column against Remy's palm vibrate. Breath rasped out of a long, powerful throat.

Remy pressed his back to the column. Part of him wanted to separate from his torch, to hide and cower in the darkness. But any beast that lived without light would be able to smell him, hear his heart pounding and sense his heat. Darkness was no shield as it was in the ordinary world.

He inched slowly around the column, but the sounds came from everywhere, echoing as they did in this accursed place. And the columns trailed off into nothing. If there were tunnels leading out of this place, he couldn't see them. He'd have to run, and hope the monster was a slow one.

He dashed from column to column. The noise grew neither louder nor softer. It was inescapable, like the heaving rumble of the sea from the deck of a ship. Remy had never been on a ship. Or had he? Inconvenient memories rose to confound him, to make him feel as if the ground beneath his feet rocked side to side, and the shadows swept around him like waves seeking to draw him under.

As he ran, columns reared up and disappeared. In some places they were broken or toppled and he ran around them. Soon he wasn't sure which direction the well lay in, if he was headed out or in, or if the monster was even chasing him.

A fallen column blocked his path and this time he stopped. He flopped down on it, chest heaving. The air heaved with him. Everywhere shadows weaved in and out of the columns and his mind tried to pluck horrific images from nothing. Blood-eaters stretched their clawed fingers toward him only to slide away, a ripple sucked backward by the tide. *The tide.* A memory of a sea journey added its terror to his mind and he clung to the grooves in the column, afraid he might be flung onto the lurching floor.

He'd been taken in the night. Loud shouts, flaring lanterns, pleads and screams. Snatched from his warm bed. Carried away from the cottage of the white lilacs and the warm arms that held him. Thrown into cold damp darkness, never to feel a loving embrace again.

"Get a hold of yourself, Remy!" he gasped. The shadows continued to ebb and flow. He bent forward and spewed out the last wee remains of his breakfast, spattering his boots. Focusing on the mess helped still the world around him. He wiped his mouth with the back of his wrist and rested his elbows on his knees, head down. "Panic induced hallucinations is what that is. That old Roderick must've stirred up the wind to get you runnin'. Probably hopes you'll throw yourself into another hole!"

The shadows chuckled. Stones falling became the clack of hooves. Deliberate steps. One. Two. A hoofed thing with two legs. If there was one thing Remy recognized it was the clatter of horse or oxen and this was no horse or oxen.

He raised his gaze just in time to see a shadow rippled across several columns. Antlers. A tall beast, walking upright. His torch couldn't catch it, only its shadow, moving sideways, circling around to Remy's left.

Trembling, he stood. He raised the torch and glimpsed a snout. Glossy fur. Black eyes. Its form was awkward and unnatural but it moved with a lumbering grace in and out of the columns. Remy's mind refused to assemble the bits into a whole. The thing appeared to be wearing clothing. It wasn't looking toward him, but down, just ahead of its steps.

It was walking the labyrinth.

Like the nuns, it didn't hesitate. Remy recognized a rhythm to the wheezing breaths. It chanted. For some reason, this terrified Remy more than anything, as if a great mystery were about to overtake him, carry him away from all he knew, never to return. If he looked into the eyes of the beast, his own eyes would be forever altered, unable to see in the light.

He turned and walked straight away across the grooved spirals on the floor. The skin on his neck crawled to have the beast behind him, but he had to get away, as far and as fast as possible. Serpents might devour him, but this thing would consume his soul.

He was gasping for air again by the time he reached the wall of the chamber. He went left, simply because it was away from where he'd last seen the beast. Finally he came to a passage, which led neither up nor down, but out, which was good enough.

He walked for hours until he could walk no more, then sank into a heap on the bare stone. He dozed fitfully, dreaming of a dark sea that spiraled forever inward toward the whirlpool at its center.

Irresistible. Inevitable. *Remy, you must go down.*

9

"Matka!" Remy cried. He jerked awake, one arm straining to reach something just beyond his grasp. He stared and stared. Why couldn't he see? Where was she? Why didn't she come and light the candle and sing sweet songs?

He sat up and raked the hair out of his face. His cheeks burned with shame. Alone in the dark crying for his *mother*? His gut ached with a longing he hadn't known since ... well, ever.

He leaned against the wall and closed his eyes. Nothing in him had the slightest desire to move. If not for the burning thirst. He couldn't even lick his lips, his tongue a dry swollen slab filling his mouth.

"*Miluji te*," he whispered, barely interested in where the unfamiliar words came from. Brain fever. Night madness. He groaned, rolled onto hands and knees, and began to creep along, snuffling for the source of one of the interminable drips. His cheek brushed against a moist patch and he pressed his tongue to it.

The coolness was a blessing, the taste not so much. He licked the stone, finding just enough moisture to keep agony at bay. "There's got to be dozens of quicker ways to die down here than dying of thirst," he said. He could drink the last of the oil of mercury and die an agonizing but swift death. "Not yet." He crawled along until his palm landed in a shallow puddle. On his belly he lapped at it like a dog. This water tasted like iron. He licked the tiny indention until there was no more. Possibly half a cup in all.

He remained stretched out, forehead resting on his crossed wrists.

Before he'd passed out, before the vision of the horned beast, before Roderick and the well, he'd been sure he was on the brink of finding his way out. He'd climbed so far. He had to be close to the surface.

His body refused to agree.

"So much easier to stay here and die." *Whine, whine, whine.* He groaned again and returned to sitting. He must live. He must avenge Glyn's death. He must save the city from the monsters churning in its bowels. Finally it struck him that he sat in total darkness and had not yet floundered about for his torch.

He saw things now. Not real things, but a distinct image of an endless tunnel was seared onto his vision. Stairs going up. Roderick's gaping leer. The horned beast. They all paraded past him on the wall he presumed was only a few feet away. Off in the corner of his mind, the woman he now thought of as his mother hummed in a quaint little cottage, poking at a hearth fire. Remy could almost feel its warmth.

This is how people die. Lapsing into dream, letting wishes enfold them and protect them from the nightmare of their reality. It wasn't a bad way to go. Better than being swallowed whole by a giant snake. Better than murder by the thing that had imprinted a mark of sheer terror on the faces of Glyn, Rosie, and the other Sir Wintervale.

Roderick was right. Lady Wintervale had unleashed a monster or two, and was planning on summoning more. With more deaths?

He crawled back the way he came, grabbling for his bone. He picked it up and after a moment, stuck it in his belt without lighting it. Time to experiment with darkness.

Walking slowly forward, he trailed his hands along the wall, ever mindful of the possibility that another pit or hole awaited him. It was slower going, this tentative groping, but somehow he felt safer, not quite so alien, his senses a tad more acute. He was becoming accustomed to the raging wind that played upon the ruins like a giant harp. He attempted to hum along, but the tune was too abstract, like when LaFey the accordion player got drunk on moss wine and pumped his instrument out of time with anything akin to music.

"Ah, sweet memories," Remy said. He stubbed his toe and flailed wildly as he fell forward, his false calm disappearing in a puff. His hands struck against stairs. Stairs leading up. His pulse quickened and he climbed. These stairs were so steep he could reach out and touch the ones in front of him, so he still resisted lighting the torch.

Before long he was gasping again, his long ago drink forgotten, throat raw, lungs burning. He stopped time and again to rest, but despite his physical misery, he was sure he'd reach daylight and pressed on the minute he could breathe again.

He started to count. Counting was something he'd learned as important if one wanted to be paid correctly, and Marek had helped him learn a bit more with the calculations for potion mixing and distance figuring. He could count to a hundred, and knew that each hundred was the same until he reached a thousand.

When he reached the ninth ninety-nine, he sat down and cursed. Then he began again. Somewhere around the fifth thirty-seven, his hand grasped air and flailed forward. Another landing. He crawled forward until his fingers scraped against a door.

"This is it. This is *the* door. Beyond this door lies the tunnel to the catacombs, the way out. Out! Do you hear me, Roderick? I'm leaving and I'm not coming back!"

He pulled out his knife, his powder, his candle and the oil. When he lit the candle the flare hurt his eyes and he looked away until he could see something other than the dancing flame. This door wasn't wood but iron, decorated with elaborate scroll work and embossed patterns in repeating squares. Instead of one bolt this door had two. A more important door. A door *out*.

Remy heated his powder and repeated the process that worked so well before. The rust took so long to give way his confidence faltered, but eventually the satisfying click of the lock was followed by the clang of the bolt. This door opened toward him, so he clung to the handle to make sure nothing struck it and sent him tumbling backward down the stairs.

Nothing except a rank smell spilled out and so he scrambled through, then set about lighting his torch. There was only enough oil left in the bottle for one more lighting. Thank goodness he wouldn't need it.

Even before the glow took hold, he sensed a vast space around him, and moving things. This wasn't the tunnel to the river. Oh, well. It couldn't be far. He lifted his torch and froze.

This couldn't be. What he saw before him was a mound of corpses. A nest of bones holding up fleshier remains on top. Snakes slithered in and out of the horror, red eyes reflecting the gleam of his torch.

"It can't be," he said. His mind lurched, suggesting to him that maybe he'd been climbing down all this time instead of up. His stomach twisted into a knot. He backed through the door, shoved it shut and sank to his knees. "No."

Tears welled and spilled over, streaking down his cheeks. Silent sobs racked him and he leaned against the cold door, letting despair wash through him.

There was no escape. No way out. He let this thought settle into his gut. He'd always expected a quick, violent death. A knife in the back, a blow from a guard, maybe an attack of the plague. Not this. At least in the king's dungeon there were people around. A scrap of food, a dribble of water.

Would he die of starvation or thirst? Would a monster get him as he weakened? Would he go insane? That might be for the best.

Not having moisture to spare he stifled his tears and wiped away snot on the back of his wrist. Would Marek sit around sniveling? No, but Marek wouldn't have gotten himself in this mess in the first place. Would he come looking for Remy? No, because he had enough sense not to wander into the catacombs. And Marek was lost himself, according to that fool crow. Remy didn't think he'd been down here more than a day or two, though it was impossible to tell. Just as it was impossible to tell if one were going up or down.

"No," he said again. If he'd ended up where he'd started, it was due to the black magic permeating every inch of the labyrinth. And where there was magic, there was hope. Even black magic could be harnessed, bent to one's will. If only he knew how. The place reeked of profane power. That's what Lady Wintervale wanted. That's what Remy needed, if he were ever to get out. He needed the damn medallion.

He stood and opened the door, taking a long look at the death pit. The first thing he'd need was a new source of light. So far the only thing he'd seen in the tunnels that emitted light were the eyes of the snakes. There were smaller ones slithering about, sliding in and out of the eye sockets of skulls, nesting in the open cavities of half-decayed bodies.

Remy hefted the bone in his hand, testing its weight. A snake's meat might be edible, its blood better than some of the rotgut wine he drank happily enough. He eased in a step or two farther, keeping an eye on the large snakes coiled at the top of the heap. His rat-hunting instincts returned in a flash and he moved quickly, ignoring the terrain of bones beneath his feet.

⁓

After vomiting until his very guts must've lay splattered about his feet, Remy concluded that raw, corpse-fed vipers were not in fact edible. Their eyeballs, however, continued to glow after death, and so the harrowing venture had not been entirely useless. He stored six eyeballs of varying sizes in the now empty vial that had held the oil of mercury. His torch gave off a scarce bit of light, and the snake eyes added an eerie red illumination to the alcove where he hunkered.

The interesting thing about the snake pit, he decided, was that somewhere high above it was an opening to the real world. An opening he had opened. Therefore, it stood to reason that he could open it again.

"And who are you to talk about reason?" he shouted, kicking aside the hacked up chunks of snake at his feet. But it did no good. He couldn't fake madness, though he longed for it. Every time he thought he could fling himself into the abyss, his mind started to work again.

First, he needed to summon Sir Roderick. If the annoying ghost wouldn't help him get out, surely he'd help him find the way to the bottom. Roderick was motivated by revenge. This was something Remy could understand. Though he'd never been very vengeful himself, he was starting to feel a keen resentment toward Lady Wintervale, who'd gotten him into this mess. He also experienced pangs of intense hatred toward Fowler, Sadie and Ollie for having the good sense to flee when he did not.

And of course there was the monster who'd slain his best friend. But harboring a grudge against a monster was a waste of energy. Monsters did what they did. They didn't have a conscience to ignore, or any sort of upbringing that might teach them not to kill. Some were greedy for gold they'd never spend, or blood to sustain themselves, or the sharp thrill of terror seeping out of their victims' flesh as they died. These things were air and water to monsters, according to Marek.

Then there were monsters who'd once been people, and might have a tiny shred of humanity knocking about their mutated brains. These were the most dangerous, more complicated and unpredictable. Like Roderick's ghost.

"Roderick Wintervale!" he shouted, and listened in irritation as his voice ran rings around the tunnels, reaching highs and lows, agitating the wind, setting the serpents to slithering. He'd retreated a way from the pit, but not too far. It was his one link to outside, like it or not.

Roderick's face emerged partially from the stone floor. "You think you can summon me at will, little beast?" he demanded.

"I just did, didn't I?" Remy would've liked to credit his alchemical abilities, but really he knew Roderick was just lurking about, waiting for the next chance to taunt him.

Roderick ignored the comment, appearing quite smug. "So you decided to heed my advice and go down."

Remy ground his teeth and balled his fists. "I've decided it is my duty to stop Lady Wintervale's evil plans. Not that I totally believe you, but clearly monsters are afoot. Give me that fool medallion so I can find my way down, and I will avenge your death."

"Haven't you been paying attention? The key to the labyrinth is etched at every juncture. On the walls, floors, even the ceiling in some places. The old ones went absolutely mad for it once they discovered it."

"Discovered? Didn't they build it themselves?"

"No one built the labyrinth. It just is." Roderick's full body came into view and he paced back and forth, a disconcerting image as he remained partially in the floor and parallel to it. Remy touched the wall behind him to fend off vertigo.

"The carvings are all different. How can I know which one is accurate?"

"They're not maps! Oh, at first the old ones tried, but seeing as how every mapmaker became irretrievably lost, the profession died out." Roderick giggled and suddenly he was standing right next to Remy. He poked at the jar of snake eyes. "I see you're adapting. Soon you'll fit right in."

Remy jerked the jar away. "If the carvings aren't maps, what good are they?"

"Take a lesson from the king."

"You said I'd never get an audience with him."

"Not that king! Not the fat and fleshy king on his false throne."

"Is there some law that says the dead must always speak in riddles? Just tell me what to do!"

"Pardon. I forget how dense the living are. You are so smothered by flesh, distracted by matters of breathing and dragging your bones around, you cannot see the obvious though it appears like a burning flame before you. Maybe you should carve out your own eyes, for all the good they do you."

"So you're not going to tell me what you're blathering on about?"

"Hearing is not knowing." Roderick pulled a mournful look, rolling his black eyes toward the ceiling. "With death comes great wisdom. Perhaps you should pray for it."

"Not quite ready to join you yet," Remy snapped. The choice to take his own life hovered like a damp raven, a dark, surly fluttering thing perched in a corner of his heart, but he wasn't about to admit that to Roderick, who would probably encourage it.

"You need to go down, Remy." Making a circling motion with a downward pointing finger, Roderick walked around him. "But the labyrinth does not abide need. Nor does it care a whit for desire, questing, noble causes, or intent of any sort. Its doors open only to where you least want to go."

"So it's hopeless to even try."

"The labyrinth hates hope most of all. Hope and light." He stopped and tapped the jar in Remy's hand again. "You must surrender to the darkness, rat boy."

"And why should I believe anything you say?"

"Keep climbing stairs until you drop dead for all I care. Then we'll have a real conversation, you and I."

Remy clutched the jar close to his chest, focusing on the red light oozing out between his fingers. He would not give up hope and light. Never.

"I'm not going to—" he stopped. Roderick had vanished in his annoying fashion. Why should Remy believe a dead man whose brains were half-eaten by worms? He talked about the maze as if it were a living thing, a living thing that existed purely to confound. If the old ones hadn't built this mess, whoever came before them must have. It hurt Remy's imagination to stretch so far back, back before giants and gods. Before light.

"Nonsense," he whispered. He experimented with putting the jar in his pocket and tucking his torch away in the folds of his cloak, letting the blackness enfold him. Without light, the hiss and moans of the corpse pit grew louder, along with the wind and the trickle of moisture.

The thought of climbing more stairs until he dropped dead sucked the last whisper of hope from his bones. Roderick had a point. Remy could not keep pushing. He wouldn't survive long without food or a real drink of water. He had to listen to the damn ghost. He had to surrender.

"Don't like it. Don't like it one little bit." He stared in the direction of his feet, but couldn't see them. Couldn't see anything except the slit of red coming out of his pocket.

He knew if he really were to give up, he'd toss aside the jar, the bone torch, his knife. Toss aside hope. He couldn't do it. Not yet.

Instead he began to walk slowly, one foot in front of the other, away from the slurp of engorged serpents, away from the hole to outside. He bumped into walls, but in time developed a sense for their presence. A vague reverberation of his breathing, the cool wet of their surface, alerted him just before he touched them.

An image of the horned beast walking the labyrinth flashed in his mind and he understood Roderick's riddle. The beast was the king Roderick meant. King of some mystic realm, meditating, calling up the power of the dark.

And the nuns, performing a rote ritual with no concept of what stirred below, chanting, calling to the very beasts they prayed fervently against in their tiny cells. Even they touched and disturbed the power below.

Remy knew no mystic chants, only spells and potions and a bawdy ditty or two. All of them were too driven by intent to impress the labyrinth. Instead he hummed the threads of a melody from long ago, the lullaby he'd last heard in his mother's arms.

10

He's worthless. Too little to be good for anything.

You said you wanted healthy children. He's healthy. Look at the flesh on his bones.

He's scrawny! He'll die a few weeks away from his mam's teat. I won't be payin' for a mouth that can't work.

Seems a shame to toss 'im in the gutter. Look at all that meat.

There are witches in the old quarter who'll pay for the bones.

Meditation did not come easily to Remy. As hope and striving drained away into the monotony of plodding through the darkness, the worst of his memories oozed in to fill the void. If the voices and visions really were memories, not just him feeling sorry for himself, making up stories. He'd never been much for stories. Glyn was the storyteller. Glyn could take a nugget of truth and spin it into the best gossipy tale, with gory details added for spice.

He wished Glyn were there to spin a story about Remy's parents.

You were born a prince, Remy. Your parents were king and queen of a distant land. An evil wizard abducted you and put a doppelganger in your place. The false Remy is ruling right now, and doing a fine job of it!

Remy never gave much thought to his parents. There was no point. He assumed they were long dead, killed by the plague or maybe in one of the battles that occasionally raged around the countryside and sometimes reached the city's walls.

But now that these memories were surfacing, a longing clawed at his heart. To think he should've been raised proper, in a house, with parents, food, guidance. It wasn't fair. And to think his folks might still be alive! He imagined them lighting a candle once a year in memory of their long lost son.

Remy became furious, and then sad, and then angry again. So angry he lost all sense of where he was and tripped over a broken chunk of rock. He sprawled on the floor, hardly registering the pain of impact anymore.

As he scrabbled to regain his feet, he felt deep grooves in the stone. *Stinking labyrinth.* If he were a great magician, he'd destroy this place. It was a canker eating away at the bowels of the city. Like a great huge tree with its guts gnawed away by termites. One hard wind and the entire city would topple.

He reached for a wall and found none. Wrapped in illusions and delusions, he'd entered another chamber

144

without realizing it. His bone torch had gone out long ago, and the glow of the snake eyes was so dim it cast him in a pool of light that didn't reach beyond the stretch of his arms. Could he find more snakes to whack in this part of the maze? He'd detected nothing living or dead since leaving the death pit, although the sensation of spiders and other creeping things never left him. And of course, the monster, always a breathing piece of the blackness behind him.

There had to be another source of light. He refused to accept blindness, no matter what Roderick said.

"What is this new hell?" he asked, stretching out his arms. For once, his voice didn't echo. The thick air swallowed it whole. Remy sniffed, then breathed deeper. The air was heavy and his lungs had to work to find oxygen in it. His head swam, waves crashed against a distant shore and he had his most vivid, most profound vision yet.

A hot, sticky pastry glowed in the middle of a spiral of strudel. Remy's dry mouth puckered as it tried to water, but couldn't. The sweet aroma of baked butter, powdered sugar and simmering fruit wafted into his nose. The taste followed. He licked his parched lips, sure a vision of such intensity would carry a few nutrients in its wake. The rich flavors settled on his tongue. The sound of a rolling pin—thunk, swish, thunk—and the sizzle of grease spattering an iron griddle transported him to his mother's kitchen. Her hands, lightly dusted with flour, gripped the handles of the pin, and she hummed.

"Turn around so I can see your face, Matka," he said. He'd never seen his mother, only sensed her presence, nestled in her warmth.

The woman turned and he was startled to see Winifred there, smiling. That wasn't right. Instead of a rolling pin she held two large knives. On the heavy wood table behind her the lump of dough turned into Glyn, cut up into several pieces.

"He tried to steal the apples for your strudel," Winifred explained cheerfully. Remy looked away but he couldn't escape his own mind. Winifred continued to chop and dice his friend into bite-sized bits, humming all the while. With the tip of one of the knives she poked at Glyn's eyeballs. They'd started to glow red. "I'll save these for your lantern, Master Remy."

"Please don't trouble yourself, Winifred," Remy said, because a hallucination was better than no company at all. Winifred approached him with a steaming hot pastry on a wooden board.

"You sacrificed him to the labyrinth. You deserve the first bite," she said.

"I didn't." Remy looked at the flaky strudel, frosted with crushed bone, leaking a bit of its crimson juices onto the board. Glyn wouldn't mind if Remy ate him. Glyn understood starvation every bit as well as Remy did, maybe better. Remy shook his head, but Winifred and her gruesome kitchen remained solid. He lifted the jar and pressed it to his forehead, driving away the vision with the red light.

Roderick said light created illusions, but Remy believed the opposite to be true. Darkness was a blank canvas begging to be painted with the colors and forms of the mind. Darkness turned him inside out, dumping his fears and memories into the tunnels to haunt him. Darkness was the enemy.

He put away the jar and blinked rapidly. A swarm of colors drifted in front of his eyes, but he refused to let them take shape. Bending down to one knee, he fingered the grooves of the labyrinth. How was he supposed to walk it when he couldn't see it? The answer dawned on him and he sat down. He pulled off his boots, and after a moment's consideration, his socks.

"I didn't sacrifice you, Glyn," he said. "Not on purpose anyway." He considered this as he tied his socks together to make a rope, which he looped through the buckles on his boots.

He'd handed Glyn his staff before summoning the monster, and had used Roderick's corpse as a shield when the thing attacked the light. *Not on purpose.* But it had served. A death to open the first locked door.

"The first strudel I ever ate was at Marek's. Solstice eve, that first winter. I was happy then. Content anyway."

He slung his tied-together boots over his shoulder, but remained sitting. "Me and Glyn used to stare through the windows at the baker's until he ran us off. Just the smell was worth getting a knock on the head. No matter how good you smell, Glyn, I wouldn't eat you. That's just the madness talking. I didn't kill you on purpose."

Didn't kill him at all. Remy never killed nothing except rats, snakes, and a monster or two. Little ones. Marek handled the big ones.

"Time to get walking." He pushed himself up, wobbling a bit. He was so hungry, so tired. He thought about the nuns, walking and chanting, and the horned beast, shuffling and grunting. Remy could shuffle and grunt. He ran his toes along the deep grooves in the floor, sliding one foot forward, and then the other.

It was too quiet. The labyrinth was a noisy place and now he heard nothing other than his pulse thrumming in his ears. A pulse that wanted to become drums, wanted to be a fist pounding dough into a fat loaf, wanted to be Marek's staff, pounding on the ceiling, signaling to him. *This way, Remy, this way out.*

But there was no out, only down. To summon power, he had to go down. Round and round and down. The stone beneath his feet was as cold as the frozen river in winter, but rough. Bits of rubble and sharp things poked the soles of his feet as he walked.

All of the spells he knew came and went out of his mind. They were no good here. The groove he followed curved slightly left before turning back on itself. This happened numerous times until he had no idea where he might have started or how many turns he took. Always there was the sense of circling, curving in and out, but never leaving the confines of the spiral. In his mind he could see the entire thing, bigger than the square in front of the cathedral. Other spirals intersected it at opposing angles, cutting straight through. Beyond endless planes of circles, stars gleamed and moons hovered, large and small, red and white and gold. The night sky had been trapped beneath the earth along with Remy.

Each object waited and watched in epic silence, mildly curious if he would fail or find the key to the labyrinth.

"The key is the medallion," Remy said. He paused, lifted his head, and continued. *Big toe follows the groove, foot down. Next toe.* Only the ground beneath his feet remained solid and unmoving—the only thing he believed for sure was real. One thing about the darkness, it did wonders for his imagination.

With every step, he sensed the ground sloping downwards. No matter how many turns he followed, the whirlpool sucked him in. A part of him still hoped, still longed to resist, to fight against the pull, to struggle. A part that was too damn tired just wanted it to end. And a tiny little snip in the back of his brain was very curious to see where this hole led, and if any power simmered in the guts of the tunnels.

More than visions of stars and strudels haunted him. The sharp bite of tar grew stronger, and raspy breathing susurrated in the deep black. The monster tracked him, maybe happy it had driven him to this place, the last door.

The slope grew steeper and Remy had to work at not losing his balance. He turned up and a few steps later, was going down again. Why not head straight down and get it over with? Because if he did, he'd end up at the beginning of the spiral, that's why. All he could do was follow the grooves. Like alchemy, and magic, this method of summoning was exact. If he exchanged one herb for another, or mixed up the order of a spell, he'd end up with unintended results. Here, going up sent him down, trying to get out drove him farther in.

Running from the monster drew it closer, ignoring it held the thing at bay. Or at least he hoped so. One by one all of his impulses and instincts dropped away, until he stubbed his toe against stone. He reached out and down. The wall was low. The edge scraped his knee.

He crouched and ran a hand along the surface. The wall was curved and about three feet thick. Water licked against rock far, far below him.

A well. Not the same well. The wall around this hole was lower. The stone wasn't rough, but smooth. He fingered carvings and gauges and guessed the marks were a type of writing he didn't recognize. People older than the old ones had built this, if people were indeed involved.

Wizards, probably, or shamans as they used to be called. Earth magic. Black magic. Remy hadn't grasped the nature of black magic before. Now he stood in its belly, waiting to be admitted. He thought of Roderick plunging headfirst into the other well and his stomach lurched.

No. Roderick was dead. What did he care if he busted his skull or fell into the open jaws of some ravenous beast? Remy might be giving up most of his good sense to the tyranny of the labyrinth, but he wasn't giving up the will to survive.

He bent forward and grabbled along the interior wall of the well, as far as he dared. Was there a barred gate as there had been on the other? Did he have enough copper powder to work a lock? But no, he had no more oil of mercury to ignite it.

If only he could see. But what good would seeing do? Even a lantern wouldn't reveal what waited at the bottom of this hole. He sat on the wall and put his head in his hands.

The quiet chamber became less quiet. The darkness breathed. Other steps dragged along the spirals. The thing was relentless, but it had to walk the labyrinth as well. It occurred to Remy the only reason he hadn't been murdered was because the monster was every bit as confounded by the maze as he was. This cheered him a little.

"Come and get me!" he shouted. The steps didn't stop, the breathing didn't alter its rhythm. The thick air sucked up Remy's words and they did not return.

He couldn't get out. He knew that.

Forcing his limbs into motion, he continued his exploration of the well. He removed one of the slimy snake eyeballs from the jar. Its glow was so faint he doubted if he could detect it under normal circumstances. He held it out over the well and let it go.

The darkness swallowed the red pinprick in mere seconds. A few seconds later, Remy thought he detected a tiny splat, as if the thing had actually hit a floor. So maybe this hole wasn't bottomless. He thought about the wells that dotted the city and remembered some of them had hand and foot holes dug into the walls to allow service workers to climb down and remove rotting animal corpses and pennies tossed in with wishes.

He reached one arm as far as it would go over the edge, keeping a foot firmly on the ground. Now would be just the time for Roderick to appear and try to startle him over the edge again. He found several divots, but none of them were convincing footholds. He lay on his belly to extend his reach, and his boots fell from where he'd slung them over his shoulder. A few moments later they slapped against stone, joining the eyeball.

"Ox balls," he muttered and continued his search. At last he found an indention deep enough to insert his toes and the ball of his foot. "So here we go then." He pushed back his cloak and considered tossing it in ahead of him to join his boots, but he wasn't that confident. There might not be another toehold.

He knelt on the wall, turned and stuck out his leg until his toes found the divot. Awkwardly, he lowered his body down, two hands grasping the edge of the well as he searched with the other foot. Sweat poured off him, endangering his grip as he squished against the wall, one leg up frog-style, the other dangling down. This was when Roderick decided to appear, glowing so Remy could see him.

"Of all the holes in the underworld, you pick this one?" he asked, one eyebrow lifting in bemusement. "Do you even know what's down there?"

"Oh, shut up," Remy wheezed, chin on the wall. Roderick sat beside him.

"You look uncomfortable. Why not just let go?"

"I still have bones that will break." Remy detected another indention and wriggled his toes into it. Gravel crumbled and fell.

"And flesh that will taste delicious to those who wait below." Roderick chuckled, clearly enjoying Remy's distress.

"I thought you wanted me to go down!" Remy cautiously removed his upper foot from its tiny ledge and replaced it with the fingers of his right hand. There was nothing convincing to cling to. "Help me or go away."

"To be honest, I never thought you'd survive this long. Lady Wintervale chose well. Why send a great alchemist into a rat hole when a rat boy will do so much better? Although by the looks of things, your luck is about to end."

"Go below and cushion my fall again, why don't you?" Remy didn't want to let go of the edge of the well, but he was going to have to, especially with Roderick tickling his fingers with his ghostly breath.

"Even I wouldn't go down *that* hole. And I'm dead!"

Remy released his grip on the edge, palm sliding along the rough flat surface. The fingers clinging to the divot instantly cramped. He lowered himself into the well, desperately seeking another toehold. His free hand found a bit of jutting rock to cling to a moment before he would have fallen.

He found another crevice for his foot, then another for his hand. He crept downward, arms and legs trembling.

Roderick leaned over the edge. "Congratulations. You might arrive at your doom in one piece."

"I would curse you if you weren't already cursed," Remy hissed. He had very little air to spare, but cursing Roderick seemed like a good way to expend it.

His tormentor laughed and displayed the medallion. "You'll need this where you're going." He flipped it into the well. It sailed past Remy and clanged loudly when it hit. Roderick vanished, leaving Remy alone with the wall and the blackness below.

His cheek scraped along the rock wall. His fingers ached from the strain. The cord holding his cloak in place choked him. Sweat ran into his eyes. He concentrated on reuniting with his boots. His toes would be happy to have a bit of cushion after this. He'd sacrifice his socks to the darkness, in honor of Glyn.

He should've done it straight away. Should've given Glyn his socks when he was still alive to enjoy them. Lot of things Remy should've done, like practicing climbing the city's outer walls. Yes, that would've been useful.

To his enormous surprise, his foot landed on a flat surface. He lowered the other and let go of the wall, stumbling backward until he fell.

"I made it, you ass!" he shouted. He rolled over on hands and knees, touching his forehead to the floor. It was damp and he heard the ripple of water again somewhere in the dark.

"Oh, thank you, gods and goddesses and what not. Thank you for not busting my spine—" Remy froze. He wasn't alone.

A wild, inhuman shriek tore through the black, and then the thing was on him. It landed on his back, claws tearing at his shoulders, teeth searching for his neck.

Remy screamed, rolled and flung the thing away. It wasn't large, but it was vicious. Hot blood pulsed out of several wounds. He snatched his bone torch from his belt and slashed the air with all his strength. He got lucky, smacking the thing as it launched itself toward him again. A solid crack rang out and his attacker squealed. It slashed at his arm and Remy lunged, punching with his fist and thrusting with the bone.

The thing, whatever it was, relented and skittered away. But it didn't skitter far enough for Remy's liking. He knew it was still there, waiting. Did it have friends? A gang?

He roared and ran toward the sound of its gnarring. It fled, and this time its scrabbling steps kept going until they faded into the distance.

Remy dropped to his knees and put his hand to his neck. It came away wet. He licked his palm. He knew his own blood would make him sick, but wet was wet.

Then he remembered the sound of water. So close. He crawled toward it, and his hand landed on a small disc. His fingers closed around the object, lifting it. The medallion. Sitting back on his heels, he let it rest on his palm. It was surprisingly heavy. He could just grip the edges with his fingertips. It had to be worth a small fortune.

Possessing it did not make him happy. Luck didn't lead him to find the medallion. The labyrinth did. He traced its spiral pattern with his finger, breathing heavily. Reward or punishment? He remained in place, rocking. Listening to the scratching, echoing, howling, dripping.

Beneath it all, music. Real music. Not like the silly lullaby that haunted him. A violin moaned out a complicated tune. As soon as his mind identified the instrument, it came to a screechy halt.

"Hello?" Remy called out.

Something scraped, like a chair, which struck Remy as ridiculous in this place of monsters and corpses.

Steps—padded, not bare or clawed—moved away from him.

"Wait!" Remy sprang to his feet. "Who are you?"

"Welcome to the bottom of the labyrinth, Remy the rat boy," a woman's voice said. The steps continued, accompanied by the swish of skirts.

Remy's skin prickled. For some reason, this soft voice frightened him more than anything so far. After a moment, he pocketed the medallion and ran after the fading footfalls.

11

REMY CHASED AFTER the steps, heedless of what he might encounter in the dark. But the way was relatively smooth and he didn't crash into any walls or trip over any rocks. The trickle of water receded but he dared not seek it out and lose his guide, as he was sure this woman must be.

He also regretted not finding his boots.

No matter how fast he ran, he didn't gain any ground on the leisurely sounding steps ahead of him. He began to fear they were another hallucination.

The footfalls began to rise, as if climbing. He slowed and put his hands out in front of him just in time to avoid colliding with a wall. He moved hastily along it until he discovered a passageway and stairs leading up.

If he never had to set foot on another stair, he might die a happy man. He sighed and began to climb, harboring no illusions that up meant out. Unlike the other staircases he'd encountered, this one had landings, and soon began to spiral, as if he were climbing a great narrow tower. An intact ruin or a sort of shaft, burrowed straight into the guts of the labyrinth? The higher he climbed, the more he fought against hope. If he did encounter a door that led to daylight, he'd die of shock.

"No danger of that," he murmured. Above, the rattle and scratch of a key in a lock was followed by the familiar squeal of rusty hinges. To his relief, it didn't sound like the door closed after his guide passed through. He ran his hand along the outer wall, but needn't have bothered. The presence of the doorway was announced by a gust of warmish air and a stringed instrument wailing softly. He paused at the opening, startled by a sense of depth and height. He squinted, trying to determine if his eyes were playing tricks again. A tantalizing glimpse of form drew him across the threshold.

A flicker of motion resolved into the partial silhouette of the woman. Remy could see the curve of her hip, the flow of her gown, the jut of an arm. The fabric of her dress gleamed as if fashioned from metal. She walked across a smooth floor and was swallowed by a deeper slice of darkness. Shadow. Shadow meant light.

Remy detected no source. His head ached from the strain of assembling hints and scraps into things that made sense: a wall, a doorway, the glint of a mirror? He hurried after the woman, pulse quickening with excitement. Here now, finally, was something.

He passed through a second doorway and stopped again. Shadows filled this room with bars, stripes and blocks. Grey layered on black, outlined here and there with a hint of silver, as if moonlight seeped in from a crack in the ceiling. And there was a ceiling, peaked and lined with thick rafters.

A sunless dream conjured by a mind unaccustomed to color. A mind stripped of light. This was death.

"Am I dead?" Remy asked, alarmed that perhaps he'd passed and hadn't even noticed, so hellish and dark was his existence.

"I certainly hope not," the woman answered. Remy searched for her and was distracted by more of the objects he thought might be mirrors. Rectangles cut a row of relief into the black wall. Not quite silver, but shiny, like the woman's dress.

He started toward them but she spoke again.

"Come. We have much to discuss."

He angled toward her voice. "Who are you? What is this place?"

"I am offended. Do you not recognize me?"

"Pardon me, Madam, but I can't see your face." Remy walked closer. She now sat on a large chair. A throne. Her strange clothing was rich and elaborate. The blend of silk and metal proved illusive to his eyes, reminding him of quicksilver. The fabric of her skirt was hard-edged, yet fluid. He pulled his gaze away from how it pooled and slid across her lap, up a torso and arms incased in a more stable sort of velvety shadow, to a regal neck and black hair spun with jewels in a tangle of curls on top of her head.

Her face was striking and hard, beautiful in a frightening way. He did recognize her, but she was much younger than last he saw her.

"Lady Wintervale?"

"You're bleeding."

"A beast attacked me. Right before—"

"How careless of you. Don't you know that blood is precious?"

"I'll stop forthwith," Remy said, and placed his palm on his neck again. The blood was sticky and didn't seem to be free flowing anymore. There was, however, a gouge in his back that pulsed warm liquid every time he moved.

"How lovely you smell. So spicy and rich with the flow of life." The lady leaned forward and Remy's skin crawled. He thought instantly of the blood eaters he'd encountered, but Lady Wintervale looked nothing like those ghouls. She in fact looked like nothing he'd ever seen before.

Not in real life anyway. Illustrations from Marek's many books came to mind. Along with being made up of varying shades of black, she didn't appear to be fleshed out, but flat. A reflection in a darkened mirror.

"Are you the real Lady Wintervale, or some type of spirit?" he asked, not really expecting any kind of answer he could understand.

"I am the real Lady Wintervale," she said with a glower. "The creature you met is but a pale remnant of what I am becoming."

"And what is that, if I may ask?" Remy remembered to curtsy stiffly, though it hurt his aching legs to do it.

"You may not. You're not ready. I must admit, Remy the Rat, I am impressed by your mastery of the labyrinth, but there is one last test you must pass before you may become my champion."

"This has been a test?" Remy's voice rose and was a little more squeaky than he would've liked.

"Once I saw you were determined to survive, I became interested in your fate. Do not think I control the labyrinth. Not yet." She stood and held up her hand. The music that had been playing softly abruptly stopped.

"Why do you play music down here, Lady Wintervale?"

"To remind me of my humanity." She stepped away from the throne, her hard and soft angles shifting, merging, realigning, as if the artist who created her, using black ink on black paper, was constantly redrawing her. Remy wanted to touch her, but of course didn't dare. "Music is the language of the heart. I do not wish to become a monster, Remy."

Too late. "Did you unleash the monster on the city?" Remy asked.

"I told you, I don't control the labyrinth and its infernal doors. The monster is an unfortunate side affect of the delve."

"The delve?"

"Some people, like Sir Roderick, enter the labyrinth seeking treasure. Others desire to see the face of the Devil, the Christian god of the underworld. You and I are here for power. Don't deny it."

Since the truth was he was there by accident, he didn't. He stood straighter, and desperately missed his shoes again. "Have you found power, Lady Wintervale?"

"Bags of it. Unfortunately, my withered shell in the overworld can't access it. We need to open the doors, and we will rule both worlds."

"Pardon me for asking, but what do you need me for?"

"Come with me." She swept her hand in a forward motion and the air around her quivered. In a flash, instead of looking upon her front he could only see her back. *Like a card being turned over.*

He followed her tall, slim form to the row of rectangles he'd noticed before. Lady Wintervale stood next to one, now facing him again. She drew aside a panel of fabric and gazed down. Remy joined her, hands itching to find out if she were made of paper or cut from cloth. Instead he clutched his hands behind his back and peered into the rectangle.

Vertigo struck him and his breath caught. The rectangle was a window, and he was looking down on a city from high above. The city. *His city.*

The long bridge across the river was unmistakable for any other, lined as it was with statues of heroes, gods, and saints. At each end the black towers squatted in their ominous fashion, and the spires and steeples of the new town spread out beyond it. There were no lights. No motion. Like Lady Wintervale and this room, the buildings were carved out of shadows, black upon black upon grey. Remy stared at the sky but could see nothing, no stars or moon, just an undulating mass that might be clouds. Might be.

"What is this?" he asked. He unclasped his hands and reached out, expecting to touch a stone wall or glass mirror, but his hand went right through the rectangle. It really was a window.

"This is the real world," Lady Wintervale said. She lifted a hand and curled it into a fist, voice hard with emotion. "The roots. The bones. The guts of the earth. Everything arose from here. The world we knew above is a mere reflection. A flower at the end of a stem, doomed to wither. Here we stand in the roots, the sleeping seed, where all power is born and returns to die."

"How do you know?" Remy asked. He thought he detected a flash of surprise in her black eyes.

"I have explored the labyrinth for a very long time. Even before I journeyed below, I knew where real power is born. Black magic is earth magic and whispers of it survive in the folklore and conjuring of the people. Alchemy is based on it. Religion is a mere froth at the surface of a churning sea and most kings and queens have no idea of the maelstrom below. You are of the people, Remy. Where Sir Roderick was doomed to fail you stood a chance, due to your humble blood. You know what it means to bow to a power greater than yourself."

"Is that what I did?"

"You submitted to the labyrinth. Most people fight it to the death. Guess who wins?"

"Lady Wintervale—" Remy hesitated. How to politely ask a lady if she might be mad? "How do I know you're even real? I've been lost for a long time. You might be a trick of my mind."

She laughed robustly, a rather shocking noise in the heavy atmosphere. "I remember those doubts. You want to touch me, don't you? Well, go ahead." She reached out an arm encased in a velvet sleeve. Remy tentatively lifted a finger, anticipating the feel of anything other than flesh and blood. And yet his skin signaled softness to him, and heat. He ran his finger along her slim forearm and found it did indeed have dimension. She pulled her arm back and grasped his hand. Fingers. Skin. A cool, smooth palm. Remy stared at the hand in amazement. The last thing he'd expected was a real woman.

He looked up into her face, and the illusion fractured. Lady Wintervale's regal countenance broke apart and the lines rearranged. Winifred Semple gazed back at him with a mocking smile.

"You see the real me, don't you? You can see through the darkness and shadows, can't you?" This seemed to please her, though Remy had no idea what to make of this new revelation.

"Winifred?"

She took his other hand and his heart raced. Here was a trap more dangerous than any he'd yet faced.

"I was once a nun. You saw them, walking the labyrinth in the chapel in absolute ignorance, unaware of its true nature. I too walked the thing a hundred times before I began to sense the power at its core, the gateway to this place. I was so dull, weighed down by all the nonsense above. Once I realized what lay beneath my feet, I began to walk the maze in earnest and eventually, I was admitted."

"You can go back and forth? You know the way out?"

Her grip tightened, nails digging into Remy's flesh. "Of course. It's easy once you discover the trick."

"And are you going to tell me the trick, or am I part of it?" He decided to take a chance and risk her wrath. "Am I going to be another sacrifice like Sir Roderick?"

Winifred laughed again. Glimpses of the real woman, the above woman, glimmered through the darkness. A vague flash of blue in her eyes, a blush beneath her cheeks. "That pest! He helped me at first but after I slit his throat in the chapel, he's been nothing but trouble. Then his brother Lord Wintervale succumbed to fear and became completely useless. You won't, will you?"

"What's left to fear? I've died half a dozen times already down here."

"Exactly. You've seen all there is to be afraid of. Now let me show you what there is to desire." She gestured toward another window, only this one had expanded to the size of a door. Deep black lines that seemed to indicate shadows trailed out from Remy's feet to the door. Lines and shapes shifted across its surface, merged and became the sketch of a man.

Remy tugged free of Winfred and the man moved his arms. Remy lifted a hand, a drop of blood creeping down his palm from Winifred's nail marks. The man raised his hand, but he didn't bleed. Remy waved, and the man waved back.

"My shadow?"

"You are the shadow, Remy. Look closer."

Reluctant but fascinated, Remy stepped toward the man. The man appeared to walk too, but didn't step out of the doorway. He was dressed in the same strange fabrics as Winifred, sumptuous and hard-edged. He wore an elaborate brocade jacket with a stiff collar, boots that reached to his thighs, and a thick belt with a gleaming sword hanging from it unsheathed. The face was undeniably Remy's. Gaunt. Large eyes full of suspicion and curiosity, sharply angled cheekbones even more defined in this aspect. His long black hair didn't look tangled and greasy but shiny and combed. A velvet cloak hung over one shoulder. The man looked jaunty, affluent and confident. Kind of like Remy pretended to be, but never quite managed.

"Quite the picture, but a little overstuffed and fancy for my taste," Remy said. He couldn't tear his gaze away from his shadow's, who looked back at him expectantly.

"Free him, Remy. We will rule the underworld together." Winifred placed a hand on his shoulder. Two of her fingertips were wet with his blood.

"And what becomes of me?" He put a hand over his heart. He wasn't ready to abandon it, even if it did thrash and send too much blood to his head.

"Why, you may come and go, like I do! Your real self lives here, and your fleshy servant does your bidding in the overworld. But we won't need them for long. With your help I will be free from my host and I will free you too."

"Host?" Realization flashed into Remy's mind. "Lady Wintervale?"

"Yes, that old bitch. The labyrinth requires many sacrifices. Rather than watch my own body shrivel away to nothing and possibly die before I achieved my goal, I attached myself to the lady. The world won't miss her."

"And what poor man is to be my host? Any old lord or knight ambling about the city?"

"No. It does have to be someone near to you, even if you don't like them much. Lady Wintervale is my step-mother, though she doesn't know it."

"And Sir Wintervale is—was—your father?"

"Yes. He stuck me with the nuns when I was born, but he didn't bother to conceal his identity when he did it. A most inconsiderate man. I don't miss him either."

"Did you kill him? To open another door?"

"The monster killed him. I don't control it."

Are you sure you're not the monster, Winifred?

Stifling his thoughts, he said, "I don't know anyone rich and powerful to sacrifice."

"Rich, no. But powerful?" Winifred propelled him along to the next window. His shadow tracked them with black eyes. *He's waiting to be born, to have access to the world of light. But for what purpose? To feed the labyrinth?*

This rectangle was again a window. Remy looked out at a confusing jumble of shapes that transformed into a mountain range. The Giant Mountains, that range of craggy peaks separating the valley of the city from the wilds to the east. A lone cart creaked along a treacherous mountain path. Remy leaned forward and the cart was suddenly closer. A sad, tired looking donkey pulled it, led by a man in a long black cloak. Before him he held out a lantern, but it did little to pierce the darkness. They moved slowly, heavy wheels of the cart catching on every rock and root in the path.

The lantern swung and lit the man's face. He was not a terribly old man, but his profession had aged him beyond his years, giving him a grizzled appearance. His eyes flashed the brilliant green Remy knew very well. Master Marek.

He leaned out the window and shouted, "Master Marek!" Was he lost in the labyrinth too? A labyrinth with mountains and paths instead of tunnels and caves?

Winifred giggled.

"He can't hear you, silly. This is merely a window into the shadow world."

"So he's not lost?" Remy sagged with relief.

"Oh, he's lost all right. I've been able to keep him in a fog to prevent him from returning to the city. He wouldn't have entered the labyrinth for me. He's too afraid."

"Too smart, you mean," Remy snapped.

"Not nearly as smart as he thinks." Winifred clasped his other shoulder and turned him to face her. Remy let go of Marek's image with difficulty. If only he could reach him—

"He has the old power. The old spells and concoctions brewed by shamans and witch women. He has black magic at his fingertips, and he uses it to drive cellar trolls from the houses of the rich. He's wasting it, draining it without a single proper sacrifice to its source."

"That's because he's not a black magician. He wouldn't spill blood to gain power."

"But you would, Remy. You sacrificed your best friend."

"I didn't! The monster killed him. You said yourself there's no controlling it."

"But it takes what you offer. It adores a hot-blooded sacrifice."

"Winifred, I'm afraid you've become completely unhinged down here."

She smiled sweetly. "No, Remy. I've become sane. Above is delusion. Below is reality. You will understand when you claim your true place. Marek recognized your abilities, and he kept you down on purpose. He used you to fight monsters and took all the credit himself. But I recognized you for what you are. You belong down here with me."

"I don't think so." He shook his head. She laid a palm against his cheek to stop him. Beneath her cool skin he detected a raging heat. She stroked him softly.

"Curse him. Curse him and take back what was stolen. All the power he's used or will ever use is yours. You will control Master Marek, the great alchemist, like a chess piece while you grow stronger in this tower. Together we will fling open all the doors, and take back the light itself. You and I, king and queen of the labyrinth."

She stepped back and his shadow stepped forward. They linked elbows and faced him, smiling benignly. Winifred was no servant girl, but royalty, with a crown of jewels on her regal head. His shadow also wore a crown. They made a handsome couple. Imperious, noble, heartless.

"How do I do it? How do I curse Marek?"

"One last sacrifice. One more maze to delve." She nodded in the direction of the chamber. Remy blinked and watched the pattern brighten on the floor. He groaned.

"Not another stinking labyrinth!"

Winifred and his shadow chuckled as he walked away from them, toward the spirals emerging from the floor. This pattern appeared to be made of marble, a weave of black and white. White! The color dazzled after so long in muted tones of black. He winced, looked away, and then back again. All he could see was the pattern, and at the center, another hole.

"Go on. Walk the labyrinth, and when you reach the center, lay claim to Marek's soul in the name of the underworld. Use your dagger to slit your wrist. Feed the labyrinth your blood. Don't worry. I'll bring you back. You do still have your dagger, don't you?"

"I do." His knife, a bit of powdered copper, the bone, a jar of spent eyeballs, and a crow's feather. He considered the feather, which had proven useless so far. The messenger crow had shed it when he delivered Marek's message so long ago.

"Once the final door is open," Winifred continued, "the medallion you now possess will lead us to the tomb of the kings. There we will claim the true throne."

He set foot on the pattern and began to walk it. At least it gave him time to think, although thinking hadn't proven very useful up to now. He had no intention of being Winifred's willing sacrifice. That shadow man might look like him, but it wasn't.

Still, the shadow's boots looked pretty comfortable. Remy's bare feet were worn raw, blisters broken and weeping. And the cloak looked warm. Winifred's hand on his arm soothing. Then Remy remembered her fingernails digging into his flesh. Not so soothing. The girl had sacrificed her heart to the labyrinth and didn't even realize it. Or maybe she did and didn't care. All she cared was that Remy offer his living blood to this last doorway, a doorway she believed led to ultimate power.

What made her think this was the last door? Simply because she'd reached a place that mimicked the upper reaches of the world above? Clearly this was a reflection of the cathedral tower. They were just beneath the bells. Above that stretched endless sky, up to where the Christian god lived with his angels, and beyond that, the great unknown. And in the labyrinth? What substituted for sky here?

This was not the bottom. It just happened to be as far as Winifred's imagination could carry her. Remy fingered the medallion in his pocket, released it, and moved on to grasp the feather. As instructed, he focused on Marek. He imagined the crow the feather had fallen from. After all, he was immersed in magic here, and blood from the Winifred-inflicted wounds moistened the barbs of the feather. Why couldn't he summon a mere crow? He, who'd conjured Marek without even trying.

Maybe there was something to Winifred's mad claims. Maybe he did belong here. Maybe that was why fate had torn him from his mother's arms and brought him to the city. Until he was ready to claim his place in darkness.

While it all had a rather nice ring to it, Remy didn't believe it. He wasn't black magician material, and he had no desire to destroy the world he lived in, for that's what Winifred's schemes would do. Open all the doors? Unleash untold monsters on the world above? Didn't they have enough trouble without monsters sucking all the light from the sky and feeding it to the bottomless pit?

Something rustled in his pocket, and squawked. He glanced over at Winifred and the shadow man, but she was back to being Lady Wintervale, flat and stiff, waiting for Remy's blood to open the door for her. She did need him. She couldn't do it herself.

A beak pecked at his fingers and he yelped. Winifred looked at him with curiosity. Remy returned his gaze to his feet and kept it there until he drew near the wall of windows and doors again. He angled away from the pattern, straight for the window he'd seen Marek through.

He reached it and pulled a fully realized, angry crow from his pocket and flung it out the window. It listed sideways as it flapped, and Remy feared it might crash to the ground far below. But it gained its balance and lofted skywards, quickly swallowed into the maw of swirling blackness. Far away, Marek plodded on, unaware of Remy, crow, labyrinth, any of it. He was merely lost in a fog. A feeble squawk reached Remy's ears, and he thought he saw Marek flinch ever so slightly.

"What are you doing?" Winifred asked. "Now you'll have to start over."

"You're right about the power simmering here. An old spell of mine finally worked. I had to get rid of it."

"You think a pebble-brained crow can find its way out of the labyrinth?"

"I don't know, but it will be interesting to find out."

Winifred's eyes narrowed. "You did that on purpose. You're giving in to fear, just like all the others. They all died you know, trying to escape."

"How long have you been here? Besides Sir Roderick, how many others have you lured to their doom?"

"Does it matter? You've come this far, why not take one step farther?" She testily broke away from his shadow's arm and strode toward him, dress clinking like tin cups knocking together.

"It does matter. You've gone too far. The music you play here doesn't reach you anymore. It's just noise, like the wind and the hiss of serpents."

"It's all music, Remy. A grand symphony playing just for me." She smiled wistfully. "You're right, you know. I had one last shred of weakness holding me back. I wanted company. I wanted you to be that company, but now I've gotten past it. I will have to kill you myself. Oh, well. There will be others."

The angles and forms that made up the chamber shifted and closed in. Lines took on sharp edges that glinted like knives.

They were knives, and they sliced the air around him. The swish of air from their movement gusted across his face. In a moment, he would be minced meat.

The windows and doors disappeared and blackness descended, growing thick. The labyrinth faded.

Remy ran toward it, dodging shadow blades, keeping his focus locked on the center of the spiral. No time for meditation. No time for anything.

As he reached the hole and skittered to a stop a blade sliced through his cloak, leaving a long cut down his back. He fell to his hands and knees at the lip of the hole.

Remy pulled out the medallion. Its spirals glowed and Remy could now make out the image of a serpent. Though it looped and twisted in the usual intricate fashion, the head ended up swallowing the tail. Both sides of the disc held the same image. The message was clear. This hole was no bottom, no final door. This was only the beginning.

Infinity lay beyond. Here, the last trappings of man ended, and the true labyrinth took over.

"Far enough," he whispered. "Nothing beyond here is any concern of mine." He held out the medallion and let it drop. It did not hit bottom before he turned away. As he reached out to crawl away from the hole, an edged shadow fell cross his hand and severed the tips of two fingers. He stifled a scream and kept crawling.

Winifred chanted incantations. Above in the bell loft, heavy brass bells whispered. He heard them every day, ringing in the dawn, every night calling monks to vespers. He heard them now. Not ringing, but vibrating as the world of shadow quaked under Winifred's onslaught of black magic.

She'll bring this place down, he thought. The labyrinth abhors hope, and Winifred hoped to kill him as a final sacrifice. Remy hoped to escape that fate. Whose intention was stronger and therefore more despicable to the darkness?

Her chanting was guttural and raw, nothing like the sweet tones of the nuns he'd seen walking the labyrinth in the chapel. Remy stopped crawling. Those nuns hadn't stopped when they reached the center. They hadn't thrown themselves into the portal. They'd kept going. They'd walked right out.

He tucked his wounded hand beneath his armpit and stood. Winifred had no blood left to give, that's why she needed him. Remy had plenty of blood, and it flowed freely now. *The monster will take whatever you offer.*

He held out his hand and blood dripped on the marble.

"Take my blood, but not my life. Take her false life instead." He pointed in the direction of her voice. He was getting woozy. Delirious with pain. Somehow he managed to find the spot where the spiral pattern left the center, and began to walk it, trying hard to surrender his grim determination to live. What he really wanted was to stop Winifred from opening the doors of darkness, so he squelched that thought too. He wanted to avoid being sliced in half. Want, want, want. He wanted to travel back in time and bring Glyn back to life. He wanted to meet his parents and reclaim the life he was meant to have. He focused on that wish, that futile hope, and kept moving.

The dark roiled and black lightning seared across the room. The thing, the beast of shadows and blades, hacked its way into the room. Winifred's chant turned into a scream.

Remy mumbled the nursery rhyme that had been haunting him. The deep timbre of the bells hummed. He imagined if the bells did break into song, the walls of the tower would crack and the edifice collapse. Winifred was wrong. This place may have given birth to the city above, but it was just a husk, a rotted shell.

There was no life here. The city of shadow was a ruin.

"The king was in his treasure house, counting up his money. The queen was in her parlor, eating cakes and honey." Remy's parched lips cracked. What a lot of nonsense the rhyme was. "The beggar sat in the square, begging for some gruel. The thief dashed among the stalls, looking for a fool."

The white lines of the pattern brightened and all else fell away into the deep black. The slashing shadow blades retreated, as did Winifred's screams and the monster's howls. The white spirals emblazoned themselves on Remy's eyes. White. The color of Winifred's soft skin. The real Winifred, who had sacrificed herself for power. The color of his mother's hands, dusted with flour.

"What I want most of all, labyrinth, is a strudel." He chuckled. He wasn't going to make it. Blood loss and hunger had finally drained him. His life energy was gone, spilled in the darkness, absorbed by the maelstrom of black magic. He staggered out of the lines, corrected himself, and kept going. Shuffling, he fell. His knees hit the marble and he curled into a ball, forehead to the floor.

Sweet voices drifted into his consciousness. The nuns, chanting. Bells ringing. He remembered it so clearly. As nice as anything to die to, he figured, though he would've preferred a rowdy song down in the public house. The chanting grew louder, the smell of incense strong enough to burn his nostrils. God's angels, coming to kick him out of God's house.

He lifted his head and blinked at the swirl of white bodies snaking in and out of the spiral pattern, circling him, drawing ever closer. Each woman held a candle, and each candle seared its flame into his light-starved brain. He raised up a little, still bent over his knees, wounded hand balled tight against his chest.

"Have you brought me a pastry?" he called out. The lead nun's gaze flickered from the pattern to the center, to him. She stopped, mouth agape, and the nun behind her ran into her back. Several nuns collided before the processional stopped in confusion. Remy giggled, eyes tearing.

"It's the scoundrel who attacked me!" a male voice tore through the chapel. Remy remained on his knees. He doubted if he could run a single step.

The chapel! Had he made it? A phalanx of monks charged him, seized him, yanked him to his feet. Their powerful hands striking him felt very real indeed.

"How dare you defile the sacred rite? To the dungeon with him!"

"Dungeon? How lovely!" Remy broke into hysterical laughter as he was dragged out of the labyrinth.

"He's mad!" one of the monks exclaimed.

"All I want is a strudel!" Remy cried, then his legs collapsed. Monks held him up by both arms. His last sensation was that of his bare feet sliding across the cool stone floor, just before he faded into sweet oblivion.

12

THE DARKNESS of the king's dungeon was no match for the abysmal blackness of the labyrinth. Remy lay unmoving on damp, rotting straw, content to not be pursued, chased, cut into bits.

Someone had brought in water and gruel, and he'd fell on it like a ravenous dog. One of the kinder monks tended to his wounded fingers, cleaning and bandaging them before lecturing Remy on his multiple sins.

All in all, life in the dungeon was good. The lanterns of the guards occasionally flickered through the bars of his cell, and their grumbling and cursing was music to his ears. Eventually he regained enough sense to appreciate the bitter irony of having escaped the labyrinth merely to be thrown into another dark hole, but he wasn't complaining.

Many questions threatened to disturb his peace, but he shoved them down. In time he might discover if Marek had escaped Winifred's fog, or if the monster had stopped murdering folks on the wharf, but for now, he didn't care. Not much.

He was still lolling in this state of utter inertia when voices reached his ears from the guard's room somewhere up above. A new voice joined in the medley, so he sat up and listened as footsteps approached and keys jangled. Lantern light cast shadows across the wall of his tiny cell.

"He's always getting himself into some sort of mischief. He's simple, you know. I've tried to take him under my wing, keep him from making trouble for the authorities, but one can't be everywhere at once, can one?"

"The monks say he's loonier than a rat with mites on the brain."

"Oh, it's quite true. But he's not dangerous."

"All he does is loll in the straw."

"Lazy. Lazy and simple. No reason to waste a perfectly good cell on the likes of him."

"You must have friends in high places to get your fool out of the dungeon, Master Marek."

"Well, the Burgomaster was quite grateful when I returned and put an end to the murdering monster. You see, the boy was only trying to help, but he got in over his head."

The voices had stopped in front of the door to Remy's cell. A key scraped in the iron lock, and the door swung open. The guard lofted his lantern, and Master Marek stepped in, nose wrinkling.

"Whatever foolishness have you gotten yourself into this time, my boy?"

Remy grinned up at him, but it was a feral grin. His heart had gone quite cold. "Did you know serpents' eyeballs glow in the dark?"

"Quite mad," Marek murmured over his shoulder to the guard.

"Best give him a good thrashing. Drive the demons out of his skull."

Marek inspected Remy with his penetrating gaze, lingering on his bandaged hands and bare feet. "Come along, Remy. You've wasted enough of my time already."

Slow and unsteady, Remy clambered to his knees, and then to his feet.

Marek turned and walked out of the cell without a word. Remy shuffled after him, and the guard followed.

"Gave the nuns the fright of their lives," he said, and Marek clucked in disapproval.

Remy climbed the dungeon stairs with difficulty. His feet ached so badly he wished Marek had left him be.

Then they exited the final iron door and sunlight pierced him to the core. He closed his eyes, unable to take it in.

"I can't walk all the way home," he said. Fresh air poured into his mouth and he breathed deeply, gulping it in.

"I suspected as much," Marek said. A donkey brayed nearby and Remy opened his eyes a mere slit. Marek's cart and donkey stood nearby, at the foot of the old city wall where the entrance to the dungeon was located. Far out of sight and smell of the castle.

Marek put a hand under Remy's elbow and guided him to the back end of the cart. Once Remy was sitting securely nestled against crates and sacks, Marek picked Remy's wounded hand off his lap and inspected it. "How careless of you. I'll see if I can craft some new finger tips."

Marek's touch, and even the stinging scent of mineral potions that always clung to him, brought tears to Remy's eyes. He didn't dare speak. The guard stood in his doorway, hands on his hips, watching them with a scowl.

Marek turned his back on the guard, and handed Remy a long black feather.

"This is yours, I believe."

"My message reached you?" Remy exclaimed.

"Imagine my surprise when the bird exploded. Luckily it did deliver its message before doing so. You must explain to me how you discovered my predicament, and how you ended up in the chapel frightening nuns, but first I will take you home and get you cleaned up. I'll buy you some new shoes, but it will come out of your allowance."

Remy glared down at his abused feet. "Glyn's dead."

"I heard." Marek's expression softened, and Remy caught a glimpse of the man who'd taken a chance on a feral boy, giving him a warm place to sleep and food to fill his belly. "Your former companions descended on me the minute I passed through the gates. I came straight away, with a stop at the Burgomaster's house. He still owes me for lifting that fairy curse, you know."

"You only just arrived? Is the monster really gone?"

"Apparently it has been inactive since your disappearance several days ago. For good or ill, people are crediting me with getting rid of the thing. You know how rumors do take on a life of their own." Marek shrugged and leaned closer. "Speaking of rumors, Saucy Sadie indicated that you'd fallen into a great pit beneath the catacombs. Tell me, is there anything beyond the old ruins? I've heard legends and old tales of a vast network of tunnels, lost treasure, hidden wells of power."

Remy met Marek's gaze. Like any good alchemist, Marek lusted after answers. After power and gold. Just the type of man the labyrinth would devour.

"No. Nothing but corpses and the serpents that feed on them."

Marek recoiled, shuddering. "How ever did you survive, dear boy? Well, enough time for that after we get you home." He patted Remy's thigh and began to move to the head of the cart. Remy caught his sleeve.

"Please, Master Marek, can we stop at the bakery?"

Marek frowned, but the corner of his lips twitched. "Of course. Vivaldi will have discounted his leftovers by now."

Remy sighed and leaned back against the sacks stuffed with herbs from Marek's foray into the Giant Mountains.

The cart clattered into motion and Remy stared up at a bright blue sky. Remy had never seen anything as beautiful as that sky.

A few puffy clouds drifted along and as Remy focused on them, they darkened. In their centers, black spirals formed, broke up and dissipated. Behind the ceiling of the sky, shadows crept, prying at cracks in the blue façade. Remy tried to blink them away, but they stayed.

The cathedral bells began to ring for vespers. *Of course.* Dusk was approaching. This was a natural darkness creeping out from wherever it lurked during the day.

Remy closed his eyes and focused on the comforting sway of the cart, and the impending delights of day-old pastry.

ABOUT THE AUTHOR

A native Oregonian, Christina Lay graduated from the University of Oregon in an age before smart phones and now works for the opera, the ballet, and a Victorian house museum. When not toiling for filthy lucre, she writes and helms ShadowSpinners Press, a cooperative authors' publishing venture. Her fiction has won several awards, including first place in the Rupert Hughes Prose Writing Competition at the Maui Writer's Conference and second place in the Writers' Digest Short Genre Fiction contest. Her novel *Death is a Star*, a contemporary fantasy, was published by IFD Publishing in 2013. Her short stories have appeared in anthologies and magazines spanning several genres. In her copious free time she enjoys sleeping.

christinalay.wordpress.com

shadowspinners.wordpress.com

The Original
DUNGEON SOLITAIRE
Tomb of Four Kings

Still Available for Free
at
matthewlowes.com/games

Complete Rules
are Print-Ready and Playable
with any Standard Deck
of Playing Cards

Dungeon Solitaire
Labyrinth of Souls

TAROT CARD GAME

by Matthew Lowes
Illustrated by Josephe Vandel

Complete Rulebook
&
Labyrinth of Souls Tarot Deck
Available at
matthewlowes.com/games

Labyrinth of Souls Fiction
Coming Soon

The End of All Things by Matthew Lowes
Littlest Death by Eric Witchey
Bayou's Lament by Cheryl Owen-Wilson
Exhumation of the Divine by Pamela Jean Herber

... and more to come!

information at
shadowspinnerspress.com

www.ingramcontent.com/pod-product-compliance
Lightning Source LLC
Chambersburg PA
CBHW021017120726
47905CB00009B/3063